A Blighted Flower and Other Stories

Portraits of Women in Modern Tibetan Literature

Compiled and translated from the
Tibetan originals

by

Riika J. Virtanen

LIBRARY OF TIBETAN WORKS & ARCHIVES

Cover photo: A Tibetan woman from 'Om bu. Photo courtesy by John V. Bellezza
Illustrations: Namgyel Dorjee

ISBN: 81-86470-27-1

Published by the Library of Tibetan Works & Archives, Dharamsala, H.P. (India), and printed at Indraprastha Press (CBT), Nehru House, 4, Bahadurshah Zafar Marg, New Delhi-110002

To my daughter Leena
and to the writers of Tibet
both inside and outside
who inspired me

Contents

Publisher's Note

Homage to Avalokiteśvara!

This book presents a collection of stories such as *A Blighted Flower* and others. The style in which the stories have emerged is not same as that of the classical Tibetan literature and hence being a new style. It is universally believed among the modern Tibetan writers that Döndrub Gyel (1953-1985) was the protagonist of this style. Be that as it may, Tibetan literature of such style began to emerge in the Tibetan society at the same time when modernisation of social aspects such as economy and political administration etc. emerged in Tibet (i.e.1980 onwards). Born in the Blue Lake region of Amdo, Döndrub Gyel was one of such writers who devoted his heart and soul in promoting literature of this style.

The classical Tibetan literature down the centuries has been greatly influenced by classical Indian style. Also there are quite a number of secular literature such as songs etc. that have emerged in a style which could be interpreted as indigenous one.

The style in which the present stories have emerged is a kind of style whose protagonists are from among those who have been greatly inspired by western culture. Such a literature first emerged in the Communist China and then gradually reached Tibet. An influence of the style that has developed under Communist regime in Tibet and China could also be seen in this literature. It may not be misleading to say that the style in which this literature has emerged is a distant relative of the style favoured by western writers.

The panorama of today's Tibetan society reveals a new phase of advancement (although not steadily) towards modernisation or rather westernisation. The young Tibetans of this phase, whose favourite choice of food lies in hamburger rather than in *tsampa,* are interested in reading English as their main source of information about Tibet and Tibetans. This collection of modern Tibetan stories presented in English translation not only reflects the visions of modern Tibetan writers, but also their perspectives towards the pains and pleasures in a person's daily life in this changing phase of Tibetan society. Hence it is a valuable source of such information for both young and old and Tibetan and non-Tibetan English readers.

The translator Mrs Riika J. Virtanen is to be complemented for devotion and hard work. She has been studying Tibetan Language and Literature in this Institution since many years and is well experienced in this field. Also she has been assisting *The Tibet Journal* as a volunteer editor. The English editors such as Ruth Sonam, Jane Perkins, Malcolm Wilson and Michael Futrell, who worked hard to improve the language fluency of this book, are also to be complemented for their valuable help.

Achok Rinpoche
Director

December 2000

Translator's Note

The idea of creating this kind of collection of translated modern Tibetan literature developed and was actualised during my tenure as a volunteer editor here at LTWA, The Library of Tibetan Works & Archives, Dharamsala. I am thankful to LTWA and to all its staff-members for providing me with such a wonderful opportunity for studies and an inspiring working environment saturated with an atmosphere of Tibetan culture and learning.

Specifically, I am grateful to the following individuals whom I would like to thank from the depths of my heart for their help and advice: my Tibetan language teacher and the Language Research Officer of LTWA, Acarya Sangye Tendar Naga, who opened for me the doors to the world of modern Tibetan literary art during his lectures at LTWA on the writings of Döndrub Gyel; the Managing Editor of *The Tibet Journal* and the Head of the Research and Translation Bureau Thupten K. Rikey, who was always there to answer any enquiries and checked the accuracy of the translations in this collection; Pema Tsering, the Deputy Secretary of DIIR, who readily shared his knowledge of modern Tibetan literature and encouraged me greatly in the beginning of this project; Ruth Sonam, Malcolm Wilson, Jane Perkins and Michael Futrell, who all edited the manuscript and greatly improved my English expression; Jamyang Dhondup, the headmaster of the Multi-Educational Center; Jamyang Tenzin, the energetic young Library Assistant of the LTWA manuscript section and Sonam Wangyel, who provided me with *pin yin* transliterations of Chinese words in the texts translated. Special thanks go to John V. Bellezza who provided the cover photo from his vast collection of photos from Tibet and to Namgyel Dorjee, the artist from TCV, who skillfully drew the illustrations.

Last but not least, I am grateful to my mother Pyry who wished to know about the life and position of Tibetan women and to Leena, who went to kindergarten while her mother was writing and translating.

Two styles of transliterating Tibetan words into Latin alphabet have been employed throughout this volume. The reason for this duality has been the need to comply with the requirements of fluency and clarity in the translations of *belles-lettres* on the one hand, and on the other hand to take into account the scholarly requirements of accuracy. In the main body of the text, both in the introduction and the translations, the names of persons have been spelled corresponding to their approximate pronunciation and the conventional way of spelling them. For example a common name like 'Tashi' has been spelled without the initial cerebral sound, because this is the usual way of spelling it, even though this sound can be clearly heard. Otherwise, in the introduction I have employed mainly the Wylie system, whereas in the translations the "phonetic" style has been employed throughout. However, in order to facilitate easy and accurate reference, in the notes and the bibliography all the Tibetan names and words have been spelt according to the Wylie system, which reflects the exact Tibetan spellings.

Introduction

This work presents translations of four modern Tibetan literary works focusing on themes involving women's lives in contemporary Tibet. Until now there have not been many complete translations of modern Tibetan novels and short stories, and so apart from those sufficiently fluent in Tibetan, it has been difficult for readers to gain access to modern Tibetan literature, except through short descriptions, excerpts or reviews in research papers and articles. The present work is intended to fill this gap to a small extent.

I have chosen to translate four stories by well-known Tibetan writers which made an impression on me when I first read them and touched me for one reason or another. The translation of Döndrub Gyel's (Don grub rGyal) "*Sad kyis bcom pa'i me tog*", "A Blighted Flower", forms the main work in this collection. It is a novella of seven chapters and is considered to be one of the pioneering works in modern Tibetan storytelling. The other stories in this compilation are: "*rGyu 'bras med pa'i mna' ma*", "A Shameless Bride" by Döndrub Gyel and Tshering Döndrub (Tshe ring Don grub), "*mGo ras kyis btums pa'i bu mo*", "A Girl with Her Face Concealed by a Scarf" by Tenpa Yargye (bsTan pa Yar rgyas) and "*dByar kha'i lo ma ser po*", "The Yellow Leaves of Summer" by Tashi Palden (bKra shis dPal ldan).

While translating Tibetan it is difficult, almost impossible, to render the original literary style and flavour of the authors in another language. Therefore, these translations remain mere reflections of the original literary works, though I have done my best to try and catch some characteristics of the individual authors' styles. In spite of the limitations I hope these translations enable the reader to gain some idea of the style, content and message of the various works presented here and to form an idea of today's Tibetan literature and of some of the more prominent writers.

All the stories in this collection focus on the life and fate of women. This theme evolved rather accidentally, as I first worked on Döndrub Gyel's "A Blighted Flower", whose main character is a young girl from the Amdo region, the native province of its author. Since I had also read and enjoyed some other stories on women's lives, the idea developed to extend this work into a collection of modern fiction linked by the theme of Tibetan women. Thus this collection offers some insights into the lives of women in Tibet, though all the stories are related from a male perspective since the stories which caught my attention happened to be written by men.[1]

The stories selected for this anthology were originally written in Tibetan. Works translated from Chinese into Tibetan were deliberately not included, as I wished to demonstrate the quite evident, though sometimes ignored, fact that there is an emerging modern literary art created in the medium of the native Tibetan language. Even though the works included in this collection were all written in occupied Tibet, it does not mean that there is no modern literature in the Tibetan community in exile. On the contrary, many literary magazines appear regularly and also several books containing stories and poetry have recently been published.[2]

On Modern Tibetan Literature and Earlier Research in Western Languages

The emergence of a contemporary Tibetan literature dates from the early 1980s, the era of liberalisation in China which brought greater leniency in Chinese policies towards occupied Tibet; this allowed some freedom, though circumscribed, for those who wished to express themselves through the literary medium. The beginning of the 1980s was marked by the appearance of several literary magazines, including *sBrang char,* "Gentle Rain" (launched in Amdo in 1981) published by mTsho sngon mi rigs dpe skrun khang (Nationalities Press of the Blue Lake), a quarterly publishing short stories, poems, critiques of literary works and also featuring short introductions to the life and works of significant earlier writers. Many of Döndrub Gyel's works first appeared in this publication in the '80s.

Other magazines which began to appear included: *Bod kyi rtsom rig sgyu rtsal* (*Tibetan Art and Literature*), *Lho kha'i rtsom rig sgyu rtsal*

("The Art and Literature of Lho kha"), *Zla zer* ("Moon Rays"), and *Gangs dkar ri bo* ("White Snow Mountain").[3] These and many other literary magazines provided the necessary podium for young writers to exhibit their talents and communicate their ideas.

In recent years some series have appeared publishing compilations of modern literature, such as the *Bod kyi deng rabs rtsom rig dpe tshogs* ("The Series of Modern Tibetan Literature") brought out by mTsho sngon mi rigs dpe skrun khang. The volumes I have read contain stories and dramas[4] which had been published earlier in various literary magazines, while some of the dramas were transcribed from television. There is also a series called *Bod kyi deng rabs rtsom pa po'i dpe tshogs* ("The Series of Modern Tibetan Writers") brought out by Bod ljongs mi dmangs dpe skrun khang (The People's Press of the Tibetan Region), in which the short story "A Girl with Her Face Concealed by a Scarf" by Tenpa Yargye was published. This story, which I have translated here, was included in a collection of his writings entitled *Byang thang gi mdzes ljongs* ("The Beautiful Region of Byang thang").

A number of articles on modern Tibetan literature have appeared in Western languages. Probably the most comprehensive overview of fiction has been provided by A.A. Moon in his three-part series on modern Tibetan fiction which appeared in *Tibetan Review.*[5] The writers of today who have received most attention from scholars are Döndrub Gyel and Tashi Dawa (bKra shis Zla ba). In her valuable article focusing on Döndrub Gyel and his literary creation, Heather Stoddard[6] also refers to works of such modern writers as Ugyen Dorje (O rgyan rDo rje), Tashi Palden, and some others, and thus provides much information on new Tibetan literary output. Mark Stevenson's article on Döndrub Gyel with his translation with Lama Choedak T. Yuthok of "*rKang lam phra mo,*"[7] which appeared in 1997, is, as far as I know, the first published translation of an entire short story by Döndrub Gyel into a western language. Pema Bhum's (Padma 'Bum) "*Don grub rgyal gyi mi tshe*" ("The Life of Döndrub Gyel") has been translated by Lauran Hartley[8] and also Professor Ronald Schwartz's translation of Pema Bhum's article on modern Tibetan poetry is expected to appear in *Lungta* sometimes in the near future.[9] In 1997 appeared an article by Alice Grünfelder on the writings of Tashi Dawa. This article, which primarily relies on sources in Chinese language, might create the wrong impression of modern *Tibetan* literature being written mainly in Chinese. Nevertheless, her article is an excellent introduction to the work of Tashi Dawa. It provides references to other sources on him and his literary production as well as information on some other young Tibetans who are using the Chinese language as their literary medium.[10] However, Tashi Dawa's works have also received some criticism from both Tibetan and Western writers.[11]

There are few earlier translations of modern Tibetan literature in Western languages. However, a collection of Tashi Dawa's works was translated into English and published by Panda Books,[12] and there is also a French translation of a collection of his short stories.[13] These works were originally written in Chinese, though some of them, like *Bod ljongs/ rgyun bu'i mdud pa la brgyus pa'i rnam shes* ("Tibet—The Consciousness Knotted to a Leather Strap") and *gTsang po'i pha rol na* ("At the Other Side of the River") have been translated into Tibetan. Some translations of poems or poems written originally in English by Tibetans have appeared scattered through various publications such as *Tibetan Review* and earlier editions of *The Tibet Journal,* and also the already deceased *Lotus Fields* which contained many excellent poems by writers such as K. Dhondup, Tenzing Sonam and some others.

The Role of Women in Modern Tibetan Literature

It is obvious that in almost any story or novel one might happen to pick up, there are most likely to be at least one or two, if not more, women characters. In modern Tibetan story-telling we find women tending sheep, working in the fields, women in love, schoolgirls, women in offices, women selling beer, in short, female characters from all walks of life are mentioned in modern Tibetan story-telling. However, the works that are discussed and translated here are creations woven around a central female character and describe her life, inner emotions and fate. Most of the stories, though not all, focus on the theme of love and the interaction between man and woman. But as each narration unfolds, we also learn about the daily life, views and dilemmas of the main characters, and many other details which to some extent must reflect the concerns that are common to women's lives all across Tibet.

Although there are writings in other styles also, like Jangbu's (lJang bu) somewhat surrealist style[14] or Tashi Dawa's "magical realism",[15] to a large extent prose by modern Tibetan writers seems to be characterised by a certain degree of realism, though often blending in a wealth of poetic imagery. However, after first saying that "literature is an art form reflecting actual life", Döndrub Gyel has written:

> Are literary images mere copies from real life or like a person's shape depicted exactly by a painter? No, they are not.... The image of a person is constructed by gathering essential features and good points from all directions and is newly-created by the writer in accordance with the subject matter and needs [of his composition].[16]

So it may be, that the writers have managed to catch in their stories—as interpreted through their own perspectives—some composite features of Tibetan women, their problems and daily lives.

What follows is a short introduction to the stories and their authors, including examples of some other works by them. This is by no means meant to be a comprehensive overview of the subject matter and it will only provide some ideas and direction for readers who might wish to go in search of more wonderful stories. If you do not feel the need to know more about the main features of these stories before approaching them for the first time, and want to retain the excitement of reading, you may now choose to turn to the actual translations and instead read the remaining part of the introduction as an "afterword."

Döndrub Gyel and His "A Blighted Flower"

In an article which appeared in *Bod ljongs zhib 'jug* in 1989, Tashi Palden wrote that Döndrub Gyel's *"Sad kyis bcom pa'i me tog"* ("A Blighted Flower") "filled the vacuum of medium length stories written in Tibetan."[17] As this work has now been assigned an important position in the development of modern Tibetan story-telling,[18] its translation occupies the major portion of this compilation.[19] Even though the life of its author, Döndrub Gyel, who is regarded as a pioneer of modern Tibetan literature, has been discussed at length by Pema Bum in his introduction to a collection of Döndrub Gyel's writings, which has been translated into English by Lauran Hartley, considering that this article may not be easily available to some readers, I have here chosen to present some basic information on his life based on Pema Bum's article and also on the prefaces and introductions in the various volumes of his Collected Works which contain some biographical information on the author.

Döndrub Gyel was born in 1953, during the early years of Chinese occupation of Tibet, in dGu rong of the gTsan tsha district of Amdo. After completing his secondary level education in Reb gong he was offered work in the Tibetan language section of the Qinghai Broadcasting Station in Siling. Recognising his ability, the office sent him for higher level studies in Beijing in the Nationalities Institute of the PRC[20] where he studied during two periods; first completing his studies in the "languages of the nationalities class"[21] in 1975, and again during 1978-1981 studying as a research student of the same institute (mainly Tibetan history); he obtained his Master's degree in 1981.[22] After completing his studies, Döndrub Gyel worked as a Tibetan language teacher for two years in the Nationalities Institute in Beijing and since 1984 in the Nationalities Teachers' Training School in Chab cha. It was here that this young intellectual, writer, scholar and poet ended his own life at the early age of thirty-two by committing suicide in 1985.[23]

Although the period of literary activity of this writer was so short, it is amazing to see how many writings in various genres he produced. In the early 80s, which was characterised by leniency in Chinese policies and cultural reconstruction after the oppression of the Cultural Revolution,[24] his writings—stories, poems, articles, translations—began to appear in various literary journals, and in 1981 appeared his first book called *'Bol rtsom zhogs pa'i skya rengs,* "Early Morning Writings from the Pillow" published by the Nationalities Press of the Blue Lake.[25] After his suicide, many of his writings continued to appear posthumously in various literary journals until the early 90s.[26] Recently, in 1997, Döndrub Gyel's writings were collected together by Bankho from the South-Western Nationalities Institute and published by the Nationalities Press in Beijing. His Collected Works (*dPal don grub rgyal gyi gsung 'bum*) consist of six volumes, each volume devoted to his writings in different genres (poems, fiction, research articles, translations, commentarial works and miscellaneous writings).

"A Blighted Flower" first appeared serialised in two parts in the literary magazine *sBrang char* ("Honey Rain" = "Light Rain") in 1982 (No.4, pp.6-28) and 1983 (No.1, pp.8-29, 47), illustrated with a snow-encrusted rose, its petals falling on deep snow. The appearance of this novella preceded by some months the publication of his poem "*Lang tsho'i rbab chu*" ("Waterfall of Youth"), which appeared in the next issue of *sBrang char* in 1983 under his pen-name Rangdröl (Rang grol "Self Liberation"),[27] and inaugurated the writing of modern free-style poetry in Tibetan.[28] The years 1982-83, when his novella was published, seem to be the years when Döndrub Gyel was a teacher in The Nationalities Institute in Beijing before he moved home to Chab cha in Amdo in 1984. However, I did not find any mention of when this work was actually written, as the year of composition and publication do not necessarily correspond. There have been three further reprints of it in various anthologies, two in the PRC,[29] and one in exile in India in pp.113-191 in an anthology of Döndrub Gyel's writings containing many of his well-known works of different genres (like "*rKang lam phra mo*" ["The Narrow Foot-path"],[30] "*Lang tsho'i rbab chu*" ["Waterfall of Youth"], "*sPrul sku*" ["Incarnation"] and several others) published in 1994 by the Amnye Machen Institute.[31] Recently, "A Blighted Flower" was also reprinted in the Collected Works of Döndrub Gyel.[32]

The central theme of the work is the love and interaction between male and female, and thus it has an appeal to readers irrespective of nationality or cultural background. The romance of Tshering and Lhakyi, a young boy and girl from Amdo province, is set in the region of Döndrub Gyel's birth and upbringing. They are both from a small village, where the main livelihood seems to be farming; several passages describe work in the fields and the daily life of an agricultural community. The small details and nuances of the everyday life of the community are described with much care. For example, the striped hem of the *phyu pa* dress usually worn by women in the Amdo region is mentioned while describing the clothing of the main character. This places the work in a category called "*dmangs khrod kyi rtsom rig*",[33] literary art of the common people, which is in stark contrast to the long tradition of Tibetan literature, most of which was composed by ecclesiastics with themes very distant from the life of nomads and farmers.

It is interesting to speculate upon where Döndrub Gyel got his ideas or found sources of inspiration for his writing. Mark Stevenson has suggested "the *zawen*[34] meditative style of Lu Xun,"[35] a twentieth century Chinese writer, who passed away some years before the beginning of the Communist regime. Döndrub Gyel must have been familiar with Lu Xun's writings. In his essay "*rTsom rig sgyu rtsal gyi snang brnyan skor cung tsam gleng ba*" ("A Short Discussion on the Literary Images"), he quotes the following words of Lu Xun on creating characters in literature:

> Creating the character of a person is not done by purposely describing one person. It is always so: one takes the mouth from Zhejiang, face from Beijing and the clothes from Shanxi, and then collects them together.[36]

In this essay, Döndrub Gyel also refers to the names of two writers from Russia and France, thus providing evidence that he was familiar with the work of some foreign authors.[37] Looking at the translations Döndrub Gyel produced, which range from poetry, prose and drama to a historical work, the source language of most of them seems to be Chinese.[38]

One young Tibetan writer[39] suggested to me that as Döndrub Gyel was working in the Tibetan section of the Qinghai Broadcasting Station, he had to make visits to outlying villages to interview people for radio, and in this way he would have acquired authentic materials for his storytelling and become familiar with various aspects of the life of ordinary people. This sounds logical. It must be noted that Döndrub Gyel's stories always depict the life of Tibetans living in the area of historic Tibet, mostly in his own Amdo region. There are no references in them to any foreign locations, *objets d'art*, etc.,[40] so we know that his stories were inspired by the lives of ordinary Tibetans, though one must add that despite the seeming "ordinariness" of peasants and nomads, the characters in his stories appear to the reader as most interesting personalities, as is of course the case with most "common" people who each have a unique personality and their own particular fate and history.

The central character of the story is Lhakyi, and the description of her agonies during the absence of her boyfriend who has gone for study and training, form the central core of the work. Thus this story also presents a portrait of a Tibetan girl of very ordinary origins, a symbol of the current generation of young people standing at the cross-roads of old and new. In the course of the events which unfold, she is depicted facing dilemmas caused by the tension between the way of thinking of her generation and that of her parents and their forefathers, which brings to the forefront the questions regarding preservation of the old and creation of the new.

This conflict between the customs and beliefs of "the old society" and "the new society" is not the only theme of the work; in relating the story of Lhakyi, Döndrub Gyel also deals with distressing human situations such as a suicide attempt and rape and their effects on this vulnerable young life.

The narrative technique of the story gives it more depth and makes it stand out among the other works of Döndrub Gyel since here the author lets the various characters, most of them relatives of the two main characters, speak for themselves. The story has seven chapters in each of which the events are viewed from a different perspective with the change of narrator. Only the first and last chapters share the same narrator, who introduces and concludes the narration. By using this ingenious narrative device, Döndrub Gyel provokes the reader with deeper insights into the events and provides the possibility of gaining more than merely a surface understanding of the reasons and motives for each characters' actions and way of thinking. By sharing the mental reflections of the characters representing the youth of today, an older person raised in Tibet before the Chinese invasion, and an elderly nun, we can gain understanding of their disparate perspectives and how these can and do lead to clashes, even in the same family.

The title of the story "A Blighted Flower," literally, "A Flower Blighted by Frost"[41] is a metaphor which is used in two connections. In the introduction a simile referring to "the frost of a merciless custom" destroying the "blossoming of youth in a young girl like a flower" can be found. Later, in the chapter titled "Lhakyi's Suffering," it says that "the stainless flower of her youth got soiled by the dirty water of a cruel rain of mud," as the story of her rape is narrated.

"The merciless custom" refers to the tradition of pre-arranged marriages which was common in Tibet. It used to be considered completely normal that parents had the right and duty to decide the life-companion and marriage of their offspring. Döndrub Gyel describes how Lhakyi's betrothal was decided even before her birth by her father and how finally she attempts to commit suicide before this marriage is to take place. This is the vehicle for the author to deal with the problematic theme of the preservation of old customs and beliefs and the situations which arise, when an individual can no longer accept or conform to their strictures. He also raises the question of individual freedom in the face of pressure from the community to which he or she belongs. The conflict between the way of life transmitted over the generations and the lightning changes in lifestyle, world-view, and environment connected with the "modern way of life" is a theme which is explored in several modern compositions.

In light of the current political conflicts facing Tibetans, there is the danger of perceiving this problem as a simple choice between the pre-1950s "traditional Tibet" and the post-1950s "occupied Tibet"; on the one hand the Chinese claim that they are trying to "develop" Tibet and banish feudal habits and on the other hand the Tibetans in exile struggle to preserve traditional Tibetan culture and arts. However, the question is much more universal, since in the modern world the "modern way of life" and new ideas are spreading globally, so probably Tibet also, even if it had remained independent, would have also been exposed to modern ways during the past half century. Therefore the contrast between the old customs and new ideas deals with the fundamental question of the relative values of conservatism and innovation.

In "A Blighted Flower", the author clearly opts for the new criticising the old. However, in the overall literary output of Döndrub Gyel, for instance in the poems *"Lang tsho'i rbab chu"* ("Waterfall of Youth") and *" 'Di na yang drag tu mchongs lding byed bzhin pa'i snying gson po zhig 'dug"* ("Here Also is a Living Heart Strongly Beating"), we can often discern a deep appreciation of the achievements of ancient Tibetans, beginning even with the legendary forefathers of the Tibetan race, the Bodhisattva Monkey and the Rock Ogress, and the heroic deeds of the Tibetan army whose "banners of fame fluttered in the sky". This is accompanied by wishes "...to bring... a new way of thinking... a new view ...", the difficulty of which the poet laments.[42]

So while the author seems to speak for creativity and against conservatism, it seems that he believed that the new arises from the foundations laid down in the past. On reading his writings, for instance the above-mentioned poem, it appears that in the case of the Tibetans these foundations are the distinctive characteristics of the Tibetan race and Tibet's ancient cultural traditions, building on which would bring out a distinctive national identity.

In his article dealing with the objectives and aims of literature to celebrate the tenth anniversary of *sBrang char*, Döndrub Wangbum (Don grub dBang 'bum) wrote that literary works should encourage the modernisation and progress of the people. He says:

> Our literary works should call unanimously for science, education and the modern way of thought.[43]

In "A Blighted Flower" Döndrub Gyel relates to the differences in thinking between the generations and not to the development of the outer environment. But in his *"rKang lam phra mo"*[44] he stands at the cross-roads of the narrow footpath and the great avenue; contemplating them, *"Sad kyis bcom pa'i me tog"* is a powerful cry for individual freedom of choice and a critique of the old customs. The problematic consequences of an arranged marriage are a recurring theme in modern Tibetan literature, which continues even now in exile.[45] Also the marriage certificate (*gnyen sgrig gi yi ge*) issued by Chinese authorities as a device for providing people the freedom to marry who they wish is prominently mentioned in many modern stories, as in "A Blighted Flower".[46]

Considering the way the author ended his life, it is interesting that this story also has a description of a suicide attempt, though the method is different from that chosen by the author who died on the morning of November 30, 1985 by suffocating from charcoal fumes.[47] It is known that he had difficulties in his social and family life and on the previous evening he had quarrelled with his wife, who then walked out on him with their daughter.[48] There are various theories as to why he took his own life and in Tibetan society different rumours circulated.[49] Heather Stoddard writes, "The general depreciation of his qualities contributed in no small way to his suicide...,"[50] but on the other hand, according to Mark Stevenson, Döndrub Gyel would have realised that he would soon be arrested, and might therefore have taken his own life. This interpretation accords with the version which Pema Tsering, a young

Tibetan writer-in-exile from the Amdo region, related to me. According to him, it was said that Döndrub Gyel had once been drinking with a friend and, in a moment of inspiration, had written a poem called "*'Di na yang drag tu mchongs lding byed bzhin pa'i snying gson po zhig 'dug*" ("Here Also is a Living Heart Strongly Beating"), which he casually handed over to his friend not intending it for publication. However, the poem found its way to a periodical called *mTsho sngon mang tshogs sgyu rtsal* ("The Folk Art of the Blue Lake"), and therefore officials would have learned about its contents and this would certainly have led to his impending arrest.[51] The poem[52] (translated in Appendix A) was in fact published in the first number of 1986 of the above-mentioned journal, soon after the author's suicide, and it contains the lines:

mi rigs kyi re ba'i rlangs pa ni mkha' la 'phyur nges yin pa dang/ gangs ljongs kyi la rgya'i sprin sngon yang lho nas lding nges yin la/ yul 'khyar pa dang gnas sdod pa'i gzhis byes kyang lhang la 'bud nges red/[53]

The vapour of the hopes of the people will surely rise into the sky.
The blue cloud of the prestige of the Snowy Land will surely float up from the south.
Those who have wandered away and those staying, the people inside Tibet and those in exile, are about to rise up.

These sentiments would certainly have been viewed as "revolutionary" or "separatist" by officialdom, as it is well-documented that there is no real freedom of expression in Tibet under the regime of the PRC, and if writers wish to express nationalist ideas differing from official policies, they have to find an oblique or disguised way of expressing them. This avoids censorship and other possibly more drastic consequences. At the end of the poem there is a date which shows it was written on July 21, 1985, about four months before the author's suicide, but it could have taken that length of time for it to reach the attention of officials to analyse it. Thus, both versions of the reasons behind Döndrub Gyel's tragic death seem plausible, since general depression and serious domestic disagreements can also lead to this kind of despair.

As for some final remarks on the location and stylistic features of "A Blighted Flower," there is an interesting remark given in parentheses on p.7 of the *sBrang char* edition explaining the word *a rgya*: "*gcan tsha'i yul skad du phu bo'i ming*"; "name of elder brother in the dialect of gCan tsha." Even though the name of the village where the story is located is not mentioned, this remark seems to hint at gCan tsha, a place located between Reb gong and sKu 'bum, which would fit well into the framework of the story as the place-names sKu 'bum and Siling are actually mentioned.

Throughout the story, the basic narrative technique of relating the events as told by the various characters, is interrupted by lively dialogues, which make use of expressions peculiar to the dialect spoken in the Amdo region, even including such minor features of the spoken language as a variety of interjections. These were the most difficult to "translate" and sometimes, due to not being able to find a suitable English near approximation, had to be left out from the translation. Also, there is a real wealth of proverbs placed in the mouths of characters which despite their function of enlivening the story, can also be treated as valuable folkloristic data on proverbs spoken in that region.

After reading the novel, I contemplated the possibility of interpreting "the flower" as Tibet and its people and their culture and "the frost" as the burden of sufferings caused by the Chinese. Also the metaphor of "a flower" has associations with a blooming of creativity, for which freedom of expression is essential. This, however, is restricted and almost frozen due to the "ice and snow" of censorship and official constraints which threaten its survival. At the end the "flower", even though it has had to undergo a multitude of sufferings, is still alive, and there even seems to be the promise of a more happy future. While we cannot know whether this kind of political symbolism was intended by Döndrub Gyel, we do know that the novel as a work of art produces a wide variety of interpretations and speaks to its readers on different levels.

On "The Shameless Bride"

This collection contains another story by Döndrub Gyel which he co-authored with Tshering Döndrub, entitled "*rGyu 'bras med pa'i mna' ma*", "The Shameless Bride". It first appeared in *sBrang char* in 1983

(No.2, pp.41-55), and has five parts which are simply numbered instead of carrying separate chapter headings.[54]

I have so far been unable to find any specific information on the life of Tshering Döndrub, the co-author of this short story, though looking at various literary journals from Tibet, it is clear that he is a prolific writer who has authored a number of short stories. Among them is "*Lam*" "The Way" which contrasts the characters of a brother and a sister—Tashi and Wangmo—as they are described by the narrator who observes them in turn. Notably in this story, a female character is created who takes an interest in literature and is diligent in her studies, in contrast to many narratives which describe seemingly-illiterate women engaged in farming and nomadic cattle herding activities. Another short story by this writer is called "*Zla 'od 'og gi zlos gar*", "A Drama under the Moonlight" which tells about a man who sends his wife to speak with the district-head to manipulate his own promotion. A somewhat longer story by this author, woven around a man called Ralo, is divided into eleven parts. Ralo has come to visit the narrator of the story, his old school-mate Döndrub, who works at the "People's Court", to enlist his help in getting back his wife who has been taken by another man. During their reunion Ralo relates the tragi-comic events of his life, which are quite colourful.

"The Shameless Bride" appeared in the edition of *sBrang char* immediately following publication of the second part of "A Blighted Flower". The story is located in a region called Brag dkar gSer mo ljongs[55] and tells the life of Küntu Sangmo, from her childhood until the early years of her marriage. As the "shameless" woman of the title, she displays no regard for the feelings of those close to her and ends up abandoning her father, husband and even her child.

Two years after the publication of "The Shameless Bride"—and shortly preceding Döndrub Gyel's suicide—an article based upon this story appeared in *sBrang char* written by Sangdren Bu (Sangs dran bu) entitled "*rGyu 'bras med pa'i mna' ma zhes par dpyad pa mdo tsam brjod pa*," "A Short Analysis of '*The Shameless Bride*'". He begins his essay like this:

> Reading the story called *The Shameless Bride* I was captivated
> by it, like watching a lively movie, and the door of my mind

was opened. It is really true to say that even if one reads this story a hundred times, one will not feel put off ... ... (Ibid., p.72)

With the words "the door of my mind was opened" (*blo yi sgo mo phye byung*) the author has caught something essential about Döndrub Gyel's writing. This quality is that his writings are no mere narration of events for the reader's entertainment but have a message and can move the reader to such an extent that he or she looks at the surrounding world with new eyes.

According to Sangdren Bu, the main topic of the story is "the new family of the socialist system and how to establish the conduct of the household".[56] Furthermore, he quotes some words of Mao Zedong about what good literature should be like, for instance about the need that it should be beneficial to the common people and be able to move and convince the people to such an extent that they will make an effort to change their environment and bring about progress in society. The author of the article further dwells upon the importance of family life for the socialist system and says that "if a family is happy, the people are happy in their minds and their courage increases. When they exhort others, there will be progress and development."[57]

However, if one reads the story, it seems to simply deal with problems of family life which are as commonplace and universal today as they were in the past, even though the family in this case is nomadic and housed together in the traditional black yak hair tent. The "shamelessness" of the main character is revealed from all possible angles, inspiring the sympathy of the reader for those related to her, and showing the repulsiveness of her behaviour. The story thus advances such ideals as respect for one's parents, fidelity between spouses and affectionate care for one's offspring. But, there is nothing peculiarly new in such values, let alone calling them as exclusive ideals of the "socialist family"; these good qualities are very normal underpinnings of family life and are encouraged as basic values almost everywhere in human society. They were also surely held as the ideals of family life in Tibet before the Chinese occupation and the imposition of socialist ideology. So, since it deals with problems typical of universal human existence, this story can touch the hearts of readers of all backgrounds.

What makes this work somewhat different in style from "A Blighted Flower", is its narration technique. Whereas "A Blighted Flower" uses the device of letting the various characters speak out for themselves, and also describes their thoughts and feelings about the events taking place, in "The Shameless Bride" a third person narrates the unfolding of events from the outside. At the same time, the narration is enlivened by dialogue between the characters using expressions typical of the Amdo dialect. The thought processes of the various persons are not revealed in much detail; instead the authors develop their *dramatis personae* through actions and words. In this way an unimpeded picture of the "shamelessness" of Küntu Sangmo's actions truly emerges, but the motives and feelings behind her actions seem to be left rather unexplored, leaving the readers to ponder for themselves any psychological depths and hidden motives in her mind.

Tenpa Yargye's "A Girl with Her Face Concealed by a Scarf"

This work was published as "*mGo ras kyis btums pa'i bu mo*" in 1995 in a collection of Tenpa Yargye's short stories entitled *Byang thang gi mdzes ljongs*, "The Beautiful Region of the Northern Plain." This was the sixth volume in a series called "*Bod kyi deng dus rtsom pa po'i dpe tshogs 'don thengs gnyis pa*", "the series of modern Tibetan writers appearing for the second time", published by Bod ljongs mi dmangs dpe skrun khang (The People's Press of the Region of Tibet). The book itself contains a short introduction to this author together with his photograph. It tells us that he was born in 1962 into a nomad family in northern Tibet, the region where most of his stories, at least those I have encountered until now, are set. Furthermore, it says that he studied in the Tibetan section of the University of the Region of Tibet (*bod ljongs slob grwa chen mo*) and was in 1995 working in the Department of Sciences (*rig gnas cud*) of Nagchu district. He uses both Tibetan and Chinese as his literary media and has since 1982 published several short stories, poems, prose compositions, research articles and translations.

"The Beautiful Region of the Northern Plain" contains eight short stories entitled "*sTag nag*", "The Black Tiger"; "'*Gyur khug mang ba'i mdza' glu*", "A Love Song with a Multitude of Melodies"; "*A che sgrol dkar*", "Ache Dölkar"; "*mGo ras kyis btums pa'i bu mo*", "A Girl with

Her Face Concealed by a Scarf"; " *'Grul bzhud kyi glu sgra*", "The Travelling Song"; "*rTswa thang gi glag phrug*", "Young Eagle[58] of the Grass Plain"; "*Rab rib kyi lo zla*", "The Vague Years and Months"; and "*rKyang rgod mdun skyod kyi dbyangs snyan*", "The Melody of the Progress of a Wild Ass". Tenpa Yargye's stories paint a picture of the life of nomads and agricultural communities in Byang thang. Occasionally some words typical of the dialect spoken in the Northern Plain are employed in the dialogues, but these are fortunately mostly explained in the accompanying footnotes. Apart from reading about the fates of the main characters in the stories, it is also fascinating to learn about life and old traditions which are still preserved in Byang thang. A good example is "The Travelling Song" which centres around a salt-expedition undertaken by male members of the community, and the traditional customs and beliefs related to it are also described in detail.[59]

Actually, both the stories "Ache Dölkar" and "A Girl with Her Face Concealed by a Scarf"[60] have women as their central characters: in the first story, two women, Dölkar and her younger sister Tshomo. However, I chose the latter short story in four parts to include in this collection as I found it more original and amusing. It is the story of a young girl called Dekyi and the story is located in two places: "Village Number Seven" on the grass plain of Nachen, and Lhasa. The author opens his narrative with the phrase, "This is a story which actually happened on the grass plain of Nachen. It is also a story which probably won't happen again in the future". He relates the story in such a way that it appears as if it were non-fiction and not a product of his creative imagination. Also, at the end of a short poem at the end of the first part of the story, he writes: "The Tibetan people on these pages—are drawn from my diary of travelling to the grass plain of Nachen."[61] It is left to the reader to decide whether this tale is based on the author's actual experiences or whether it is a story in the normal sense of the word, and even whether the author—who is referred to as "Teacher Tenpa Yargye" by the characters in dialogue, is only using his own involvement[62] as a narrative device that enlivens the story and gives veracity to its seeming absurdity.

Tashi Palden and His Work "The Yellow Leaves of Summer"

Tashi Palden is a productive writer in the Tibetan language with several short stories, articles, poems and at least one full length novel to his credit. There is some information on him in Heather Stoddard's 1992 article on Döndrub Gyel, which says that he was born in 1962 in Rin spungs, near Shigatse. Furthermore, he was said to be working then as a reporter for *Bod ljongs nyin re'i tshags par khang,* Tibet Daily News Publishing House.[63]

In 1992 his first novel appeared under the title *Phal pa'i khyim tshang gi skyid sdug,* ("The Joys and Sorrows of An Ordinary Family"). This seven hundred and two pages long work describes the life of Tsheten Lhamo and her family, and also those somehow related to her or her family members, over a time span of more than thirty years. Through the medium of this extended family, the reader becomes familiar with the daily life in an average agricultural village in the gTsang region of Central Tibet. This is all described in meticulous detail interwoven with the changes that came about during Chinese rule in Tibet; totally alien agricultural policies like the establishment of communes (*kung hre*) and the difficulties that accompanied this. In short, the work is written in a very realistic style, devoid of any breath-taking flights of imagination or psychological insights.

Tashi Palden is the author of several short stories[64] including *"gNyen sgrig,"* "Marriage," which deals with the popular theme of marriages arranged by parents against their offsprings' wishes, and then there is *"Sems nad,"* "Anxiety," which is narrated in the first person by a teacher called Rigpel who recounts the problems and feelings of guilt surrounding a teacher's dishonesty while correcting examination papers, and also explores the emotions of loyalty and respect a student can feel for his teacher.

As for his articles, there is for instance the research article titled *"Don grub rgyal gyi brtsams 'bras dang des bod rigs kyi rtsom rig gsar par thebs pa'i shugs rkyen skor"*, "On Döndrub Gyel's writings and their influence on modern Tibetan literature," which appeared in 1989 in the scholarly publication *Bod ljongs zhib 'jug.* It is a lengthy composition of twenty-one pages and forms a good introduction to the literary output of Döndrub Gyel.[65]

The story translated here is entitled "*dByar kha'i lo ma ser po*," "Yellow Leaves of Summer" and it appeared in *Bod kyi rtsom rig sgyu rtsal* (*Tibetan Art and Literature*) in 1996 (No.2, pp.28-48). It was written in Lhasa in November/December 1995, this making it the newest literary work in this anthology of translations. The story's sub-title reads: "The third story on the theme of baby-sitters" (*bu rdzi ma'i brjod gzhi'i gras gsum pa*), indicating that two other stories by the author on baby-sitters had appeared previously. Both of them were also published in *Bod kyi rtsom rig sgyu rtsal* and are titled "*Yig 'bru gcig kyang med pa'i 'phrin yig cig*" ("A Letter Without a Single Character") and "*Dri yi bzhon pa*" ("Wind"), the first telling about a young girl who is baby-sitting for others and missing her home and the second about a baby-sitter who vanishes, suspected of having robbed the house of her employers, and is later found with a big scar on her face selling vegetables.

"The Yellow Leaves of Summer", which is the lengthiest of this trilogy, has nine parts and is located in an unspecified town, thus forming a contrast to the works of Döndrub Gyel, Tshering Döndrub and Tenpa Yargye included in this collection which all take place either in villages or nomadic areas. The story suggests that many young girls living in the countryside dream about moving to town, even if they have to drop their schooling and work as baby-sitters for their relatives or acquaintances there.[66] This theme can also be discerned in Tenpa Yargye's story in this collection, where a young man speaking to the narrator mentions girls not feeling attached to the grassy plateau and wanting to go elsewhere.[67]

In "The Yellow Leaves of Summer" the main character of the story, Nyidröl (Nyima Dölma), is sent to town to baby-sit at a very young age for her elder sister who is working in an office and has two children and a husband. The central theme of the story revolves around an illicit relationship developing between the main character and her sister's husband, and the narration creates such depth to the story that the reader can understand the feelings and mental states of the characters and feel real sympathy for them as the events unfold.

The title of the story "The Yellow Leaves of Summer" has many associations. At the end of the eighth part of the story (p.47 in the Tibetan original), we read:

... suddenly she felt something light fall on her head. When she reached up for it and looked it was a yellow leaf ... Even though the entire tree was bent with the weight of its profusion of leaves, the sparse leaves growing on one thin branch had turned yellow ... she felt very sad and thought, "Why are there yellow leaves in this season?"

Any interpretation of the metaphor of the yellow leaves growing on a thin branch, while all the other leaves of the tree are still green, is left to the reader, but it suggests to me that the author is using the leaves turning yellow before their time, in full summer when everything should be verdant, to symbolise a girl whose life has been spoiled and so, deprived of the pleasures of youth, has "withered" before her time. Another association could be that the yellow leaves suggest she will become a nun, as earlier in the story she says she would rather take robes than get married with the older man being pressed on her by her elder sister. After this scene she goes missing and it occurs to those who are searching for her that she might have disappeared to become a nun. However, the end of the story is left open, so we do not actually learn where Nyidröl has gone, whether to become a nun or whether the yellow leaves will soon turn brown and flutter to the ground, suggesting that she takes her own life.

—The Translator

A Blighted Flower

❖

Döndrub Gyel

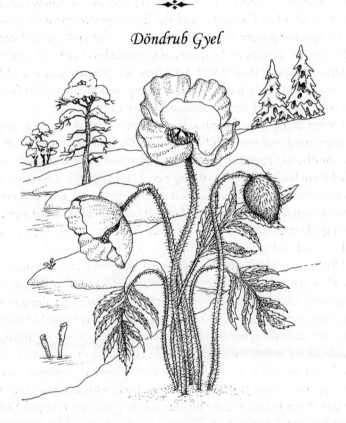

Tshering's Words

Every time I remember these sad and distressing events, a torrent of tears flows uncontrollably from my eyes. An ocean of suffering whirls around in the depths of my pure soul and the wind of my love whips up spray from the waves of my anguish, scattering them heavenwards. Isn't it true that twenty-four years of worldly life is a story blending both happiness and sorrow?

Lhakyi and I were like small flowerbuds maturing in the same garden. Our souls were connected as if the same by one thread of life, and we were as close as this since early childhood. The petals of our love unfolded and the flowers of our affection for each other bloomed together. But, this young girl's blossoming youth, zest for life and hopes for the future were suddenly destroyed by the frost of a merciless custom. I, the bee, who had hovered round the flower, with attachment, sank into an ocean of misery. Generally I have no wish to tell this sad story, but because of the repeated requests of my elder brother I will relate its beginning, hoping that it will help free our parents and the older generation from the trap of deluded thinking, and so that at least future generations will not have to suffer as Lhakyi and I did.

Lhakyi and I were neighbours and, since there was only a single wall separating our two families, we were the best of playmates from early childhood. Together we arranged plates of heaped stones[68] and offered them back and forth as if they were Losar gifts. We also competed as to who was most clever and skilful at creating horses, asses and other creatures from red clay. Sometimes I played father and she played mother, showing affection for each other. At other times we played happy games like hide-and-seek and tag.

During our childhood Lhakyi and I were very close, as fond of each other as brother and sister. However, my elder brother Rigyag and Lhakyi were like a dog and a goat together; they didn't get along at all. Sometimes, when my brother was teasing her, Lhakyi turned to me for protection and taking her side I would wreak "revenge" on my brother. He didn't have much patience and I always used to tease him. I even forced him to call me "elder brother".[69] One day, without saying anything, my mother beat me all over my body with her fists. She said later that it was for teasing my brother. Lhakyi saw me crying and said: "Elder Brother,[70] don't cry. If Rigyag doesn't call you 'elder brother', I will call you 'elder brother' from today."

After that, she called me "elder brother" and I considered her as a sister.

Oh, when I recall those events of my childhood I feel real delight and happiness. Though childish, our two minds, free from delusions, blended as one like water mixed with milk. Over the course of months and years, Lhakyi and I turned into adolescents and the petals of the flower of our youth opened wide. Now every time Lhakyi called me "elder brother" she appeared uneasy, and when I responded to her I felt I had moved on. After that our relationship started to develop in a new direction.

I'd completed my elementary education and was preparing for entrance examinations to the Malho Nationalities Teachers' Training School. My father was very supportive and advised me to work hard at my studies, shaking his finger to emphasis all the advantages and benefits that would follow. I was very happy with this, thinking that my father's concern was only for me and that he held me dear; only later did I understand that there was another motivation behind all the things he told me.

"Well, now the time has arrived when you two brothers 'don't have to ask advice from your father and beg food from your mother.[71]' It's high time to take a wife; in fact it's really overdue." My father said this one day, after we had had our supper, and we, our father and us his two sons, were sitting drinking tea.

He continued "However, the elder is Rigyag. It's a custom of us Tibetans that the family property will be taken care of by the elder. Tshering ...," father threw a glance at me and continued, "As the more clever of you two brothers, it's best if you can engage in studies. If you cannot make it you'll have to be a groom,[72] " he mused.

Father became lost in his thoughts. A victorious smile arose on the face of my elder brother. I had just turned fifteen years old and, thinking that father's speech was ridiculous, I started to laugh.

Father saw me laughing and he tapped the nape of my neck, saying:

"Now, if you are like a young eagle your wings are strong and agile. If you are like a young fish your swimming skills have developed. Now go, go, go. It is time for you young eagle to soar in the sky and time for you young fish to swim in the lake. Educate yourself well and there is nothing better than that."

I had done well in my studies at the elementary school and I was confident that I would pass the examinations. The question papers were quite easy and so after taking the exams I was admitted to the Malho Nationalities Teachers' Training School. When I was about to leave for the school all the people of our village, young and old, came to escort me. In the midst of the crowd was a young girl who was staring at me with tears in her eyes. You must surely know who that girl was without my explaining. I also loved her and felt I couldn't separate from her. However, as I also held a resolve to receive an education dear, with my mind filled with sorrow and biting my lower lip[73] I started on the road to Rebgong Sermojong.[74]

Malho Nationalities Teachers' Training School is located in Malho Prefecture. Immediately on entering the gates the visitor inhales the fragrance of aloewood blossoms.[75] On both sides there is an attractive fenced orchard of fruit trees. Regimented lines of lofty eucalyptus border all the perimeter's four sides. Viewed from afar they resemble a platoon of soldiers uniformed in greenish-yellow and standing to attention in formation. Many species of trees grow in the orchard including pears, their crowns heavy with the burden of fruits, and when they sway slowly in the cool and soft autumn wind, bowing their heads this way and that, it looks as if they are welcoming the new students arriving from all directions.[76] Flowers such as aloewood-blossoms, lotuses, grass-lotuses,[77] irises and small and big lilies displayed their white, yellow, blue and red faces and, as if they were competing in good-looks[78] as young maidens, one more attractive than the other, they smiled in a graceful way.

This is how I became a student at that school set in a beautiful environment. I took to my studies like a thirsty person who wants water or a hungry person who wants food. After making a continuous effort, which was like the flow of a stream, I finally achieved good results in my studies. Unfortunately, during the following summer vacation I fell seriously ill. I had to stay in bed at home for over three months and became weak and my condition became so serious that my mind couldn't control my legs. My parents thought that there was only one chance in a hundred that I would survive and they really suffered. I also thought that during this lifetime I wouldn't be lucky enough to continue my education and considered myself very unfortunate. Luckily, my illness could be cured by medical treatment. However, since my health was still not so good and also because the tiredness had not yet left me, I still had to stay at home and rest.

Over half a year passed like that and the principal of my school informed me that he considered that I'd dropped out. He even sent my registration certificate and other documents to our commune.[79] Now,

I had become a labourer carrying a basket[80] on my back; my karma as an educated person wielding a pen had been exhausted. Even though I suffered mental agony at that time, what could I do? Then, 'healing my own mind' and gritting my teeth, I joined the labourers of our community.

As I had not done this kind of physical work for many years, the first twenty days or more I experienced many hardships. The upper part of my body was aching and my legs and hands hurt. In the area of our community there are many passes and slopes and it was really arduous to climb up and down these mountains. During that time Lhakyi took great care of me and made it as easy as possible for me by carrying my shovel, basket and other things on the way to and from work. However, she was like the crown jewel among all the girls of our community, the young men buzzed around her like bees around a flower. They didn't leave her side even for a moment, like a body unable to separate from its own shadow. Relations between Lhakyi and me gradually became more and more distant.

One day, when work was finished and I was coming home I felt tired and rested, squatting on a small rock. Two rough hands stretched round from behind me and covered both my eyes. Instinctively, I knew that they were the hands of a young girl. But there were calluses on those industrious hands, from that I could tell she was a capable female. After a while she withdrew her hands and everything turned bright before my eyes. It was like emerging into light from a dark hole. When I turned and looked it was Lhakyi. Her hairline was like a sliver of the new moon on the third day of the lunar month and below her eyebrows, shaped like a raven's outstretched wings,[81] there were two intelligent eyes shining like the reflection of sunlight on water. They were like the eyes of a wild animal, confident of their ability to pierce through the secrets of others' minds in a single moment. Her cheeks were youthful and shone white and red, beautiful and alluring like ripe apples. The striped border of her gown was slightly torn and threadbare and through it one could actually perceive her natural gracefulness, which proved the lie in the old adage of our forefathers that "Clothes make a man."

"You are such a feckless boy. When you take a wife, later, you will be ashamed in front of her," she said to me playfully.

"It's none of your business. There's no reason to worry. Better to run after the young men and you're sure to fulfil your aims," I said with a hint of irritation.

"How can one catch a golden fish in an ocean of jealousy? Didn't you hear the saying, 'You need tolerance to be chief of a village. You need a long rope to lead an untamed horse?'"

"I'm not a chief taking care of a village. I'm also not a servant leading a wild horse. It's all right for me to be intolerant. It's all right if the rope isn't long. What does it matter to you?"

"Although a tiger leaps through the forest it rests in a den; and although a vulture soars high in the sky, it alights on a rock. Don't you need a lair for resting or a rock on which to land?"

"Oh!" How true the saying is that inside words there are words and inside bone there is marrow. I couldn't say anything in reply. Before, even when she was surrounded by young men, if she got a chance Lhakyi would hurl some words at me that were like stones, or cast a darkly-veiled glance at me. My goodness! The secrets of a girl's mind are like a muddy puddle. If I were a water-purifying jewel I could clean away all the delusions. But I'm not the jewel *ketaka*.[82] Anyway, an affectionate female fish was circling around the iron hook of my love. Was that an auspicious sign or an omen that I would not be successful? A wild animal that has run into a snare can't escape and also a female fish that has been caught in a fishing net can't be free.

However, as before, like crows following a hunter the young men of the community were circling around Lhakyi. Especially Lhündrub, who was very handsome and also from a wealthy and powerful family. He took every occasion to tease Lhakyi or to lead her on by helping her in any way. When I saw or heard these things I always felt uneasy. Actually, this was the real reason for breaking off my friendship with Lhündrub. Before, Lhündrub and I had been good friends. However, now when our paths crossed we avoided each other like people who are strangers. Anyway, he was a competitor whose assets were many times better than mine. This is why I felt very afraid that my relationship with Lhakyi wouldn't continue.

Occasionally I thought that since there were many girls in our village, why should I be attached only to Lhakyi? Even though her appearance was beautiful, she was not to be revered like an object of offering. Over the course of months and years she would also be marked with ugly wrinkles. Although she was so shapely, who could tell what her mind was like? Usually the minds of beautiful girls change like the weather in the three months of summer. Just after the sun shines there is rain. When it is still raining a rainbow appears. When the rainbow has formed it thunders. Immediately after the thunder there's lightning. I thought that it would be better to search for a girlfriend whose temperament was agreeable to me. However, the bee of my mind's love escaped uncontrollably to the petals of Lhakyi's bloom. Now I had no control over my mind and I was helpless.

In summer, when the sun was about to hide behind the western mountains, my elder brother showed me a silver ring, saying, "Tshering, you wait, today I will give you a present[83] ".

As he emphasised the two syllables of the word "pre-sent", I knew that the matter was significant.

"Whose ring is it?" I asked, even though I thought that it was most probably Lhakyi who had sent it. My elder brother said laughingly: "You know exactly who it is from. Come here."

He pulled at my ring finger and forced the silver ring on it, saying: "The size is right."

Oh, this isn't only a silver ring, but it's a present symbolising affection and meaning that a young girl's knot of love will never be untied. Thoughts about life, happiness and yearning for love suddenly entered the citadel of my mind like a cat pouncing on a mouse, or like a hunter anticipating his prey. The seedling of yearning for love between male and female, fertilised by the hope of sharing the good and bad things of life, and protected by the sun of affection, opened its leaves and started to grow for the first time on the fertile field of my pure soul.

However, when my brother told me that Lhamo had sent the ring, my mind froze and I could neither eat during the day nor sleep at night. It is true that Lhakyi and Lhamo are sisters. However, the girl I was attracted to and had fallen in love with was Lhakyi, not Lhamo. Anyway, I was thinking that I should try to return the ring to Lhamo, but as no chance came up I couldn't give it back for some time.

One evening, when my brother and I were sleeping in a small wooden hut, he suddenly spoke to me. That day there had been a powerful argument between Lhündrub and Lhakyi. My brother didn't really know what had caused the argument, but Lhakyi had threatened Lhündrub with the words: "Don't you have any shame?" to which Lhündrub shot back, "Even if it means me remaining a bachelor all my life, I wouldn't take a girl like you as my wife."

Thinking about this, it is possible to guess the subject of their argument. At that moment I felt slightly better, but Lhamo's ring was still with me and I couldn't sleep at all during the whole night.

Only later, when I gave the ring back to Lhamo, did I understand the matter completely. In every way the thoughts of Lhakyi and I were exactly the same, but nobody except Lhamo knew about our relationship. I didn't confide in anyone, even my elder brother.

At that time, Tashi, the secretary of the commune, came to give me a message. Starting the very next day I would rise to become a staff member of the commune. He said that as I was good at paperwork, and also knew a little Chinese, I would work as the veterinarian of the commune. I told him that I wasn't trained as a vet, but he responded, "It doesn't matter. We'll send you for intensive training to the veterinary school at Tongkhor. Our commune's in an area that's both agricultural and nomadic so our main livelihood comes from cattle-rearing. Therefore Doctor Li is not enough. To know more, come to the commune tomorrow and Doctor Li will fill you in."

This auspicious news spread all through the village. Next day, when I left for the commune, Lhakyi followed me far along the road. I thought that she'd come to keep me company but when I told her it was time to go back home she said that she was coming all the way to the commune to fetch a marriage certificate. I told her that I had only just become staff and since I still had to go to study in Tongkhor it wouldn't be a good idea to get a marriage certificate. Her eyes filled with tears and she said, sobbing, "Now you've been made a government employee, you can't stand the sight of someone like me?" I explained to her in many ways that it was not like that and swore that whatever happened my mind would never change. Only after that did she turn back, hesitantly, looking repeatedly over her shoulder.

I studied at the veterinary school in Tongkhor for two years and when I returned the sad events had already taken place. Far from the pain of relating these events to you, simply remembering them is a cause of unbearable suffering. So, readers, please be content with my relating this much.

Lhamo Reveals Her Heart

My name is Lhamo, Lhakyi and I are sisters. We were also companions growing up side-by-side, playing and laughing when we were young. As is said in an ancient Tibetan proverb: "Boys of the Tiger Year are rare. Girls of the Dragon Year are hard to come by." The animal of Lhakyi's birth year was dragon. Both from the point of view of her inner qualities and outward appearance she was a crown jewel among the girls in our community. The young men gave her the nickname Sengcam Drugmo[84] ("Lady Lion Dragon"). Some of them called her Yithrog Lhamo[85] ("Charming Goddess"). From the time she turned fifteen there was an unending stream of suitors. However, Lhakyi's father was stubborn and when he said something, even if he later discovered it to be wrong, he didn't admit his mistake. He clung to his prejudices. His guiding principle was, "A Good man keeps to his word and a dog to its track." One of his favourite sayings was, "A dog does not eat iron and a man does not eat an oath."

When Lhakyi was still in our mother's womb, my father and Akhu Nyima had a secret conversation. That was the reason why he didn't give Lhakyi to any of those begging for her hand. However, for a long time Lhakyi had in her heart a boyfriend who was dear to her and whom she could trust. She hid who she was thinking about even from me, and didn't disclose it for ages. Before I used to think that Lhakyi probably meant to marry Lhündrub, but then after they had a violent quarrel I realised that my thoughts had been totally mistaken.

I don't have good looks like Lhakyi and also my character is not so honest. No young men of my age were asking for my hand and, lastly, very few of them were even teasing or joking with me. However, because relations were good between me and Lhakyi, some young men were flattering and trying to please me while holding another goal in their minds. As I was able to understand Lhakyi's thoughts, the number of those trying to please me increased further. Every time I secretly related the hopes of those young men to Lhakyi a smile arose on her face, but she only shook her head and said nothing. However, that shake of her head was like pouring icy water onto the hearts of the young men. Actually, some young men do not have any dignity at all. Some made their requests like watchdogs, bowing their heads and wagging their tails even if their requests were doomed. There were also those who got

angry. Regardless of whatever method they used—soft or harsh—
Lhakyi's mind was steadfast like Mount Meru, unchanging like a *vajra*
rock mountain. At that time circumstances forced me to deceive my
own sister who was also my close friend.

One day, Agya Rigyag silently gave me a flowery scarf inside which
he had placed a half kilo of sweets and said, "Try to give this to Lhakyi."
I even told him, "I can't give it," but he insisted and because he was
honest, and because I felt compassion for him when I saw his expression,
I promised to fulfil his wish. A smile spread over his face, but when he
turned and went I thought that Agya Rigyag's hopes for Lhakyi were
like a frog who lives in a dark hole but whose mind has wandered to
Lingkar Töd.[86] That evening, carrying Rigyag's present, I went to Lhakyi
and using something else as an excuse I called her to the door saying,
"Lhakyi, there's a present for you today too. It's true that if you're
beautiful you get lots of presents."

She said in a slightly irritated way, "You don't have to do these
things which are not your duties. I don't want these dirty presents. If
you want you can take it."

"If you don't want it, the Chinese will. If I don't give it rumours
will spread.[87] Don't regret this later."

"Eh, wait for a while. Who has given this?"

"If you don't want it, never mind who it is." When I was about to
leave she grabbed my braid and asked, "Dear sister, tell me the truth.
Who sent it?"

I pursed my lips and gestured in the direction of Tshering's house.
But since the night was dark Lhakyi did not understand my gesture
and said, "Tell me quickly, sister, dear. If you tell the truth I'll give you
a reward."

"What will you give me as a reward?"

"This." Lhakyi poured all the sweets from the scarf into the front
fold of my *chuba*.

"It's a bit improper if I eat all the sweets given to you. Somebody's
heart might ache over it. I'm sure you'll regret it."

"It is really true that 'Before people come to think about something,
it has already arisen in the minds of ghosts.' Speak the truth. I won't
mind."

"It's someone from the family next door."

"Is it Tshering? Could it be? Dear sister, don't tell anyone else."

I gave all the sweets back to her. Next morning, when we went together to fetch water Lhakyi had tied Rigyag's scarf round her head. Even though I understood that she had fallen for my lie, I acted as if that scarf had been given by Tshering. I was on the verge of disclosing the deception, but I didn't dare to. Anyway, I thought that as Tshering and Rigyag are brothers what difference could there be between them, so I stayed silent. She gave me a handful of sweets and said, "Since you are the bridge and the middleman between us two, this is your share." On the way she told me many things about how nice and handsome Tshering was and now and then took the scarf off her head and waved it in the air. Sometimes she put the scarf inside the pouch in the front of her *chuba* and pressed it tightly against her chest. What she did was exactly like a small child who's been given a nice plaything.

"Sister, what do you think of Tshering?" We were on our way home, carrying water, when she suddenly asked me this.

"Tshering? Tshering from which family?" Although I understood what she meant, I pretended I didn't and asked like that.

"There is only one Tshering, how could there be two? Don't be so obtuse."

"Oh, Tshering? I don't have anything to say. He is clever and good-looking. If he isn't considered good, then who could be?"

Although the air of the summer morning was cool, a pink flush spread over Lhakyi's face and a stream of warmth flowed into her heart. She was unable to suppress her happiness and hit me with her fist with full force, which caused me acute pain. Because she hit me so forcibly, water spilled from the container on my back and splashed her neck. As her body was warm, steam rose from the nape of her neck.

When we got near the village she took out a silver ring and gave it to me. With an embarrassed expression on her face, she said, "This is my answer. The love of a young girl is entrusted in it. Sister, give this to the right person."

At that time Tshering had recovered from his illness and was labouring. I thought that I should look for a suitable moment during the day's work and try to give him the ring. However, at that time the women had to do weeding and even though some of the men were watering the field, Tshering was not among them as he had just started to work. Therefore, for some days I didn't find a way to give the ring to him.

Rigyag was watering the field, and when he noticed the flowery scarf on Lhakyi's head he smiled and used every opportunity to speak with her. Sometimes he helped Lhakyi weeding and when the work was finished in the evening, and it was time to go home, he took the initiative and did whatever he could like helping to put the weeds she'd collected into Lhakyi's basket. Although I was silently laughing at that, I acted as if I didn't know anything. Because Lhakyi kept asking whether I'd given the ring, I felt pressure to accomplish the task. Since it was just the beginning of the second round of weeding there would be no chance to meet with Tshering for at least a month. When I was thinking what I should do I got a new idea.

One morning, when Rigyag was alone watering one long rectangular field, I pretended I had to attend the call of nature and went to Rigyag. "Agya Rigyag, come here! I have something important to say," and with these words called him to the edge of the field where we couldn't be seen by others. There I reminded him how I'd helped him before and said, "Now you have to help me". He said delightedly, "Of course I'll do it. Tell me quickly."

"Try to give this to Tshering." I behaved as though the ring were mine and gave it to him with an expression of slight embarrassment. He stared at me in a dubious way and said, "I can give it, but I don't know whether Tshering will accept it. If he doesn't accept it then don't put the blame on me."

"He has to accept it. If he doesn't want to wear it, he can give it back to me. But don't bring it back personally. You must make him return it. Do you understand?"

Laughing, Rigyag put the ring in the fold of his *chuba* with the words, "That will be easy."

The weeding was finished. The green crops were waving back and forth in the soft cool wind and the branches of the apricot trees at the edges of the field were laden with fruits yet to ripen. Soon the green crops would turn as yellow as gold. When autumn arrived there would be a heavy workload harvesting, threshing the crops and collecting the grain in the granaries and so on. As usual, after the weeding was finished people rested for three days. During that time they slaughtered an animal to improve their diet. That day I had to boil the meat and Tshering had to wash the intestines. As it wasn't possible to boil the meat before the intestines had been washed, we also helped to wash them. Carrying a copper pot of lukewarm water, I purposely went over to Tshering. He smiled at me and said, "Will you help me?"

Holding a bloody intestine, he said, "Well then, let's go. Go over there." When we had reached a small rock where there were no other people, he said, "Was it you who sent me a ring a few days ago?" as his hand removed the muck from inside the bloody intestine.

I thought that I had to test him and I nodded my head as if it were really so.

"It is really kind of you to hold me in such affection." He threw a glance at my face[88] and as he didn't see any expression of uneasiness, he went on while cleaning the intestine: "However, ha, ha!", he laughed and seeing his expression it seemed as if he did not recognise me, "To tell the truth, I have a girlfriend."

"Oh, who is your girlfriend?" I deliberately asked him.

"I haven't told anyone yet. Even if I don't tell you, you'll certainly come to know later."

I pretended to be miserable and remained silent. Tshering also didn't have anything to say and he stayed motionless for a while. Then he dug down into the fold of his *chuba* and took out the ring. He bent his head and with his left hand threw the ring in front of me. Though it was difficult I made a big effort not to laugh. I didn't take the ring. Then he suddenly lifted his head and said, "Here,[89] take your ring."

"Though you've been given a silver ring, it's your loss if you don't wish to wear it. Don't regret it later."

He glanced again at my face and now there was a slightly irritated look in his eyes and an expression of dislike.

"I don't have anything to do with that ring. If you don't want to wear it, give it to Lhakyi. Why are you giving me the ring that belongs to both of you?"

He stared at me in doubt. Looking at the expression on my face he gradually withdrew his extended hand and looked carefully at the silver ring. He then put it back in his pocket. He smiled at me and said, "Don't be angry". "Ts...ts..., I really am angry. When you serve me piss instead of tea, do I still have to laugh? I definitely won't be friendly with a person like you after this."

"Don't be like that. Later I will tell you all my secrets."

Just then I noticed that Rigyag was approaching and when he saw that Tshering and I were talking he quickly changed direction and went away. After that, as soon as Rigyag saw me he would tell me news about Tshering and ask me about things related to Lhakyi as much as he could. I used to feel compassion for him from the depth of my heart, and as the empty hopes of his childish mind were so at odds with the actual facts, it seemed somewhat ridiculous. Although I more than once thought of speaking with him honestly, the love which he had for Lhakyi was sincere, and his wish for her so evident that I didn't want to say words to him which would be like dousing icy water on a mind afire. On the other hand, I'd caused him to be misled and felt a tremendous sense of regret.

Anyway, my way of perceiving Rigyag had undergone a change, and if I didn't see him for a day my heart felt empty. If my true love for him could purify the sin of having deceived him, it would not be improper even if I spent my whole life serving him. However, Rigyag's logic had been completely obscured and he wanted to wear an untouchable rainbow. All his mental focus was concentrated on Lhakyi. I didn't have a hook which could have caught his mind. Now what would happen would happen. I put my hands in my sleeves and there was nothing more to do except watch the show.

One day a very good occasion arose and I hinted to him that his imaginings were only empty hopes and that even though the rainbow in the sky is beautiful it cannot be worn as a dress, and even though the female tiger in the forest is brave it's not to be kept as a watchdog. However, he said to me, "If there's no horse in an innocent mind then there's no need to carry a bridle inside one's sleeve."

"Have you heard about the fur of a turtle and the son of a barren woman? The horse in your mind is like them."

I tried to open the door of Rigyag's mind in every possible way, but the door of his intelligence was secretly sealed with an impenetrable lock which couldn't be opened, as if it had rusted and tarnished. Speaking nicely with Rigyag was like explaining Buddhist teachings to the ears of a wolf. Therefore I thought that if I didn't play a trick on him he wouldn't wake from his stupor. Then I exchanged a scarf which father had bought me for Lhakyi's old scarf, pretending that Tshering had given it to her, and tied the old scarf round my head. This time Rigyag's intellect was really sharp. Immediately he saw that I'd tied the scarf he'd given to Lhakyi round my head, he again and again asked the reason.

"What need is there for so much investigation? Don't you see that there's a new scarf on Lhakyi's head? If a yak doesn't want to drink water the worst thing is to force it down by the shoulders. I don't need a new scarf, and as I don't have even an old one I took this scarf for myself. What is so strange about that? If you can't give it up, here, take it back."

As soon as Rigyag heard my words he snorted and quickly turned away.

I thought that the present strategy had been successful and that now nobody would cause harm secretly and create obstacles for them. I thought that those two affectionate pure souls, bound from before by the knot of love, could now be as one without being separated for even one moment. However, later I understood the stupidity of what I'd done.

After Tshering had gone to study in Tongkhor, Lhakyi didn't want to eat during the day or sleep during the night, and she fell into an ocean of suffering. Her face turned greyish-yellow and the flesh on her body became emaciated. She was like a patient suffering from a liver ailment who'd been confined to bed for some months. The separation from Tshering caused an incurable illness in her heart. Unfortunately,[90] during that time a lot of different rumours spread through the village. Although there was no basis[91] or essence to the rumours, if Lhakyi had chanced to hear them she certainly wouldn't have been able to tolerate it.

The poisoned arrows of those baseless rumours pierced the passages of my ears more than once. I tried by every means to keep them a secret from Lhakyi but, as the proverb says, "Fire cannot be enclosed inside paper," and those nasty rumours also reached her ears.

"Sister, it would be better to die right now than become Rigyag's wife."

"Lhakyi, it's as if their mouths are on fire. If you are innocent in your own mind, what need is there to be afraid of the Lord of Death?

As for those whose tongues should be cut out, let them say what they want. You don't have to listen to them."

"Sister, that scarf ..."

"Oh, that scarf? Tshering gave it to you. Don't heed them. Let them say whatever they want." When she asked suspiciously about the scarf powerful regret arose in my mind. Though it caused me unbearable suffering, I didn't have any choice but to continue lying.[92]

"Anyway, those rumours in the village are harmful to me. In the end even both my parents will believe them. All we can do is pray for the next life because Tshering and I do not have the *karma* to stay together in this lifetime. Ohhh..." There was no energy in Lhakyi's voice. The rims of her eyes brimmed with tears and she was sighing again and again.

No matter which way I tried to console her, her suffering heart could not be calmed.

On the third day of Losar that year Rigyag's father Nyima went to Lhakyi's house carrying "the beer for requesting the bride's hand".[93] Lhakyi's father said to him, "A good man keeps to his word and a dog to its footprints. A dog does not eat iron and a human does not eat his oath. Generally, this girl of mine is worth a hundred gold coins and a thousand silver. Though her price is a hundred superb horses and a hundred strong *dzos*, firstly, because of your kindness in saving my life, secondly, because we two are blood brothers, no property worth a cent is needed. However, since Lhakyi is my eldest daughter, the marriage celebration must be done elaborately."

This is how it was decided that Lhakyi and Rigyag would fetch a marriage certificate on the fifteenth day of the new year and the marriage celebration would be on the fifteenth of the fourth month.

As I hadn't seen Lhakyi since the third day of the new year, I felt uneasy. On the eighth day I purposely went in search of her. Her face was the colour of ashes and she was standing by the door looking completely drained. After we'd spoken briefly about family matters and the new year we started to talk of her marriage.

"As Rigyag is an honest man, there's no reason to hold a grudge against him." After a while she said, her eyes filled with tears, "Lhündrub must be behind the rumours that have spread in the village. Lhündrub's mouth is silkier than milk and his mind is sharper than a thorn, and since I have disappointed his hopes he holds ill-feelings towards me, so when we had the argument he said, 'You evil spirit, look out. I'm not a man if I don't take revenge for this'. He has spread those rumours out of ill-will towards me. However, my mother has also been deceived by this nonsense and father, too, is saying, 'During the whole of my life I have never held any grudges against anyone and I have obeyed the principle: The best man keeps to his words and the dog to its track.' Now, when you and Rigyag have become close by yourselves without discussions, it suits my wishes like a running horse. To get married is the *karma* of all lay women. Which girl would want to stay all her life by her mother? Now it's time for you to get married.' My father is a stubborn man and it's useless to plead with him."

Lhakyi, wiping the tears away with her left sleeve, continued, "Whether good or bad, I do not dare to disobey my father's order. However, I don't wish at all to be Rigyag's wife. Sister, now there's no other way than to die."

Seeing her withered body, grey complexion and how the tears fell one after another from the two sunken eyes in her head, I felt enormous compassion for her and was very angry with Rigyag. Then I quickly got up and went to look for Rigyag.

"You shameless old dog!" I called to Rigyag from the door and threatened him, "Do you think that snatching your younger brother's wife is being a hero? Evil spirit, can a person like you be counted as a human? Have you not heard the saying, 'If a human being does not have shame, he is a dog. If a dog does not have a tail, it is an evil spirit?'"

Rigyag was amazed and shocked and for a while embarrassed. On his face there was an expression of incomprehension. "Lhamo, if you have something to say, say it clearly. Who has snatched his younger brother's wife?"

"You. You're not even ashamed. Ask yourself."

"Ah..., me?" He was even more astonished than before, saying: "Hah, hah, haa! Don't talk nonsense."

I looked at him angrily and he shrank like a bird which has seen a hawk. Looking at him it seemed as though he'd become paralysed. Then I explained to him clearly about the relationship between Lhakyi and Tshering and in detail about how I'd deceived him and Lhakyi. He was astounded and stared at my face with startled eyes.

"Evil spirit! You evil iron-lipped spirit!"

Rigyag beat his chest with his fists and rushed into his house. His curse on me was accurate and apt and I fully deserved it.

I don't know very clearly what happened after that. However, after a few days Lhakyi and Rigyag were enjoying each other's company like a body and its shadow. I thought that Lhakyi too was being insincere. Every time Rigyag smiled at me I naturally felt disgusted and depressed. Anyway, a change took place in the events after this which was completely beyond my comprehension and Rigyag and I became very friendly and inseparable. As I cannot relate those events clearly, please now listen to Rigyag's words.

Rigyag's Illusion

In my opinion my name Rigyag ("Good Intelligence") which I was given by my father doesn't match reality. Since childhood I've been a person of dull mind. Although my younger brother Tshering is two years my junior, there's a difference like earth and sky between the intelligence of us two brothers. It is really strange that such a difference in intellect can come about between two brothers of the same paternal lineage, born from the same mother's womb. During our childhood, when we went to school, my younger brother was so clever that he went up one class every year, from first to second, from second to third and so on. Even though I read the books for three years, I couldn't pass the class one exams. So my father said to me, "Rigyag dear, it's not your destiny to read books. Hold a shovel. I think that will suit you better."

That is how I stopped learning letters and began holding a shovel becoming a labourer. If I analyse the experience I have gained during my twenty-six years in this world, cyclic existence is like a revolving wheel of miraculous appearances. Whatever happens, good or bad, I don't want to pay attention to it. As I don't call things either good or bad the girls and boys of the village say that I am an honest person. Although father always threatens me, and calls me a fool, I don't care about that. If I think about it, father is not to be blamed. I am the oldest son, and according to Tibetan custom the oldest son has to take care of the family property. Father has doubts that I will be able to take care of our heritage. Honestly, I am not a fool. Especially as I have been born as a man, I do have a sense of dignity.

My father had already disclosed to me that I was to marry Lhakyi. However, as Lhakyi was like a lotus blossom among the flowers and a moon among the stars, many men were requesting her hand and associating with her. Lhündrub, especially, had a clever mind and also his family was well-off. If I were to compete with them it might turn out as it says in the proverb, "A fox cannot reach the place where the tiger jumps." If it were like that, I would lose my self-esteem. I really didn't know about the relationship between my younger brother and Lhakyi. I can swear to that. But equally, I can definitely say that my younger brother did not know that Lhakyi had been promised as my wife and that I had also tried to win her.

While I was waiting for a suitable occasion, like a gift from heaven it happened that Lhündrub and Lhakyi had a quarrel and became like a dog and a goat. Though I felt immensely happy, I didn't show my feelings. That evening I thought that I should explain my secret to Tshering. However, when I told my younger brother that Lhakyi and Lhündrub had quarrelled, he made no comment except for laughing in a way that suggested he didn't think anything about it. Therefore I kept my secret in my heart. Then, although there were some young men trying to please and flatter Lhakyi, and though I competed with them, I felt sure of victory. So I arranged for the flowery scarf, which I had bought before, and a half kilo of sweets to be given to Lhakyi through Lhamo.

When I saw Lhakyi wearing that scarf on her head I thought that my hopes had been fulfilled and felt inexpressibly happy. But who could have known that Lhamo had deceived me? Though during that time Lhamo kept trying to tell me something in many different ways, I didn't know that her words were a hint, and even though she showed me many different hints, I didn't take any notice. She sent a silver ring to Tshering, and when I saw Tshering and Lhamo whispering secretly while preparing the meat I thought that they had a relationship.

After Tshering had gone to Tongkhor to study, when I saw the scarf which I'd given Lhakyi wrapped around Lhamo's head, I felt strange; and as Lhakyi was wearing a new scarf, I couldn't help feeling suspicious.

During that time Lhündrub told me many personal matters and I also confided my secrets to him.

"Friend, these days young girls can't be trusted at all. Their minds change like lightning flashing in the sky and their insides are filled with deceit like the inside of a white shell filled with worms. So it is better to take the matter into your own hands and declare it to all the young and old men and women in the village."

"I haven't yet asked Lhakyi's consent. If we act like that ..."

"You foolish black-mouth.[94] Isn't it a sign of consent that she's wrapped your scarf around her head?"

"Then, how ..."

Lhündrub again interrupted me: "Haven't you heard the saying 'A pig needs a snout. A human being needs intelligence?' You can leave that responsibility with me. If I can't make it known to all the villagers, men and women, young and old, by tomorrow dawn, I, Lhündrub, am not a son of my mother nor the foal of a mare."

Really, Lhündrub has an amazing ability to create rumours. Next day people were exaggerating, adding two to one and a thousand to a hundred, about how Lhakyi and I had got acquainted, how we had talked together, how our minds had become close and so forth. Those events were such that let alone not imagining them in my mind, I hadn't even dreamt them in my dreams.

Anyway, those rumours spread everywhere in the village, and my father, taking the opportunity, asked for Lhakyi in marriage and Lhakyi's father happily gave her as my wife.

However, after Lhamo explained the matter clearly to me, I felt deep regret and an unbearable suffering arose in my heart. That evening I explained the situation clearly to my father. Though I requested that the marriage between me and Lhakyi should be called off, my father said, laughing: "Oh, that's really strange. But what difference is there between you two brothers? Moreover, you are the oldest son, and there is no custom of the younger brother getting married before the older brother. As your old uncle has a fierce character, he won't be delighted if we change things around. Because Tshering is commune staff the young girls will certainly be crowding round him. You are more important. Now the wishes of this old man have been fulfilled."

The minds of the elderly are more inflexible than seasoned wood and tougher than stiff leather. There was nothing I could do about that. I thought that I would have to achieve my aims in some other way.

The twelfth day of Losar arrived. There were only two whole days left till the day when Lhakyi and I were to fetch the marriage certificate. My heart was turbulent like the waves of an ocean. At teatime, on the afternoon of that day, I saw Lhakyi walking with heavy steps towards the village barn. I thought that this was a suitable opportunity and followed her. I was thinking that I should speak with her and tell her exactly what I had done wrong, that we would not go to fetch the marriage certificate and would use all means to wait for Tshering's return so that they could marry.

After she had vanished behind a small hill on the way to the barn I followed her, pretending that I was going for a walk. The barn was behind the hillock in a vale and normally people only went there to tend the horses and asses. I wondered what could Lhakyi's reason be for going to the barn today? I got alarmed and quickened my pace. The door of the barn was slightly ajar. I heard a strange sound coming from inside, like the sound from the throat of an old owl. I quickly opened the door of the barn. Oh god! A red belt was dangling from the beam. The end of the belt formed a noose and it was round Lhakyi's neck. Her face was turned upwards and the eyes were bulging. Her tongue was stretched out and her whole body was shaking. What had seemed like the sound coming from the throat of an old owl was actually coming from her throat. Gradually, the duration of that sound got shorter and shorter and its pitch got lower and lower. Now there was no time to think. I quickly took out my knife and slashed the belt. As soon as I had done that this girl, half-dead, fell heavily into my lap. My whole body kept shaking. The hairs on my head were stiff and the hairs on my body were also standing on end. Not conscious of how I'd released the knot from her throat, I massaged her chest with quivering hands.

After a while her breath became regular again, and the colour gradually returned to her face. Looking at my face with her two half-open eyes, she said, "You are to be blamed for this."

I couldn't say anything except shake and nod my head. My eyes and throat were choked with tears.

"If I am alive, I am a human being who belongs to Tshering. If I die, I am a ghost belonging to him. I do not want to be your wife."

The veins in her eyes had all turned bright red and the two eyes in her face gave me the feeling that a big blaze was consuming my lungs and heart. Though I deeply regretted my earlier deeds, I couldn't say a single word to express my regret.

Quite a while passed like that, I then completely confessed to Lhakyi all that I had done and the way I'd behaved. I told it all to her exactly, without hiding anything. When I had explained to her at length how Lhamo had played tricks and how Lhündrub had spread rumours and other things, her anger slowly subsided and a look of embarrassment spread over her face. Then I made her promise that she wouldn't tell anybody about her suicide attempt and we discussed how we would reply to my father and her father.

From the next day Lhakyi came happily to my house and I also went to her house and stayed there, having a good time. During those days both our fathers were in a good mood and in the evenings they were drinking *chang*[95] together and talking. But they didn't know about the secret discussion between Lhakyi and me. Only then I understood what Lhamo had meant, and although I sometimes secretly smiled at her she didn't pay any attention to me at first. But after Lhakyi had given her a slight hint about our secret discussion, she also became close and affectionate with me.

The fifteenth day of the New Year arrived. Lhakyi and I went happily to fetch a marriage certificate from the commune. When we were setting out many people joined us and Lhündrub came up to us with a deceitful smile on his face. He said, "Friend, as it is said, 'Don't forget your lama when you are successful in your monk's life; and don't forget the go-between when you are successful in your marriage.' So when you come back from the commune, don't forget to bring a gift of *chang*."

"I'll bring you a gift of piss."

I was at a loss for a reply to him, Lhakyi said this and Lhündrub stuck out his tongue and laughed.

When we left for the commune Lhakyi and I went together. On the return journey it was not known where Lhakyi had gone and the one who came with me was Lhamo. My father looked at the marriage certificate and frowned deeply. Inside me a ball of yarn of laughter was secretly bouncing up and down.

However, I didn't have anything whatsoever to do with Lhakyi's escape to Labrang.[96] She herself is completely to blame for that. Lhakyi is a shameless woman. Young men, please ask Lhakyi herself whether she has any shame or not.

Lhakyi's Suffering

It's due to Rigyag's kindness that I can still enjoy life in this world. If he hadn't saved my life in that hay barn, I would have departed from this world. Rigyag can't be blamed for calling me a shameless person. I've engaged in every kind of immodest activity, and even though I regret that, how could I help it? Rather than doing that it's better to recite some *mani*-mantras[97] to try to purify all the stains of my sins. Though I sometimes consider becoming a nun, Tshering's face, the affection of our childhood and the attraction of our youth appear vividly in front of my eyes like illusions conjured by a demon.

Generally, I too would like to enjoy normal life like the girls of today, but my appearance became my enemy and I couldn't stay with my kind parents, nor was I able to be together with the friend who was close with me. If Tshering had collected a marriage certificate when he was about to leave for Tongkhor, these wrinkles of suffering would not have marked my pure heart. What the proverb says is really true: "Although girls' hair is long their minds are short." It is likely that these words apply to many young girls. In any case, I am like that.

After Tshering had gone for his studies in Tongkhor, many kinds of rumours about me spread in the village. My mother spoke a lot of good things to me about Rigyag, praising him highly, and my father, without listening to my pleas, stubbornly brought the matter to a close. Before, in the old society,[98] my father had gone out to do trading and when he was returning he met three bandits on the road who robbed him of his valuables. They tied him to a tree and meant to kill him with a knife. At that moment, Nyima, Rigyag and Tshering's father, took out his knife and came running without any concern for his own life. The bandits got frightened because he also had a gun over his shoulder, and they escaped hastily on horseback. As my father's life had been saved, and he hadn't even lost his valuables, my father and Uncle Nyima swore an oath of friendship. In the year of the Liberation[99] they both had reached their thirties. This also happened to be the year of their respective marriages, which took place on the same day. Next year Tshering's mother gave birth to Rigyag and a year later my mother also became pregnant.

One evening Uncle Nyima came to our house and the two blood brothers reminisced about past events while drinking *chang*.

"If you hadn't arrived just at the right moment I would have gone to meet the Lord of Death," my father said after taking a gulp of *chang*.

"Those are past deeds. There's not much point in speaking about them. Blood brother, I have a plan in mind. But..."

Akhu Nyima looked at my mother's face and, slightly uneasy, stopped speaking.

"Say it! Say! What could there be to keep secret between us two brothers?"

"It is so. It is so. I think the same. Hm...hm..."

As Akhu Nyima couldn't speak out, my father glanced sideways, slightly irritated, and from his expression it appeared as though he was reproaching his friend, as if to say, "If you don't trust me, you don't have to say it."

"Ha, ha...," said Uncle Nyima with a forced laugh, "To be honest, I thought of suggesting a connection by marriage to you. As you know, I have a son. As Wangtsho too is expecting, if a girl is born please give her as a wife to my son."

"Hah, hah, haa! You blood brother! Though I'm hoping for a son, you wish for a girl. If it's as you say, I'll certainly give her to you."

"Is that like 'A good man keeps to his word and a dog to its track'?"

"Sure. It's definite. A dog does not eat iron and a man does not eat an oath."

Just like that my father decided on my marriage before I had even arrived in this world. However, I didn't know anything about those events. Even the only one I could trust, my mother Wangtsho, didn't drop any hint. On the third day of Losar, after father had given me as Rigyag's wife, I appealed to my parents as I cried. Mother caressed my head and related the above discussion to me. Oh dear, is the fate of a girl like that? Though it would be difficult throughout my whole life to repay the kindness of my parents, why is it that I am sent on a path to death irrespective of my own feelings and wishes? Reflecting in this way I felt disappointed in my parents and developed a wish to escape from cyclic existence. Whichever way I examined it, I couldn't relieve my mind from the ocean of suffering and on the afternoon of the twelfth day of the New Year...

Now, when I remember those events they have become a cause of sadness, of regret and shame. Rigyag spoke a lot of consoling words to me and we three, including Lhamo, discussed our views of the situation. Finally we decided that on the morning of the fifteenth day, Lhamo would go ahead of us to wait in the commune, while I would catch a bus to Siling from the road so that I could go and see Tshering. When I wished Rigyag farewell he gave me twenty *yuan* and said a lot of good and kind words to me, such as I should behave well while on my way.

Since I hadn't left my birthplace before, I felt happy sitting on the soft and comfortable bench of the bus. When I heard people chattering in various languages that I couldn't understand my mind felt empty and the talking made me bored. As the journey proceeded, they also got tired and some of them fell asleep, lolling to their right and left. Some were looking at the scenery outside the windows of the bus. The past events of my happy childhood arose like a film on the mirror of my mind.

In the sixth month of summer the crops had grown green in the lands and fields surrounding the village. When the soft cool breeze gently touched them their movement resembled the swell of the ocean's waves. Grasshoppers and birds were chirping sweet melodies. Butterflies and other winged insects were dancing in the air and from a faraway place a cuckoo was singing his sweet song. From the southern horizon a white cloud tinged with black was hastening northwards. After a while a light rain fell gently and a rainbow of five colours appeared in the sky. Many tiny dewdrops had formed on the leaves of the crops and other plants growing there.

"Agya Tshering, rainbow, rainbow!"

Pointing my finger towards the sky where a rainbow had formed, I was running towards the place close by where it began.

After a while, Tshering slipped ahead of me. No matter how hard I tried to reach him, I couldn't catch him. I pretended to cry and Tshering ran back and consoled me. Then hand-in-hand we went to catch the rainbow. When we arrived at that valley the rainbow was on the other side of the mountain and gradually faded.

"When you cried just now, Lady Rainbow got annoyed and returned to the heavens. In future when a rainbow appears, don't cry. I'll try everything I know to catch it."

I acted as if what Tshering had said were true and nodded my head. I waited for rain and the coming of a rainbow. However, though it rained many times, after that I didn't see a rainbow.

The hooting of the bus horn awakened me. Tears were filling my eyes uncontrollably and I felt depressed. The rumours in the village, Rigyag's scarf, Lhündrub's threats, father's stubbornness and Tshering's face were like a strong flood forcing its way into my heart.

"Friend, where are you going?" Suddenly a young man sitting beside me asked me this. As soon as I heard the Tibetan language being spoken I was delighted. He was wearing Chinese clothes and on his wrist there was a watch. Because of this he looked like a government employee. However, from the grease on the collar of his Chinese clothes, the grime on his hands, his thick fingers, and the dirt under his nails he seemed to be a farmer. Anyway, I felt comfortable having a Tibetan as my travelling companion. He asked me a lot of questions and I also told him that I was on my way to Tongkhor. However, I didn't mention even one word about the suffering in my mind. According to what he said he was from Rebgong and was now on his way to visit Kumbum monastery.

On the way he gave me a lot of sweets and fruits. When we arrived at Siling, he took me to a hotel and treated me very nicely. I thought that he was a kind person. Next day, he gave me a bus ticket and said: "Today there's no bus to Tongkhor. I've bought you a ticket for tomorrow. In case you would like to visit Kumbum, we can go together."

I thought that as my travelling companion was nice I could visit Kumbum. I asked him about the price of the bus ticket to Tongkhor, to which he replied in a nonchalant way, not accepting my money: "As we are from the same region, there's no need to worry so much about a few *yuan*."

He also paid for the bus ticket to Kumbum.

At that time religious ceremonies had just started in Kumbum and there were a great number of pilgrims. He was well acquainted with the monastery and he explained to me about the many marvellous statues there. I paid them my respects through the three doors of my body, speech and mind.[100] I didn't however understand his real intentions. In the afternoon, when the sun was about to set, he said in amazement, "Oh, now something has gone wrong. The bus to Siling has already gone. What should we do now?"

He quickly looked again and again at his wristwatch. As I had to leave the next day for Tongkhor, my mind got agitated and became like a flaming fire.

"Don't worry. It's no more than thirty kilometres from Kumbum to Siling, so it's near. Today we've spent all day paying our respects in the monastery and haven't even had any food. You must be hungry. Now we'll look for a restaurant, and when we've filled our stomachs we'll go on foot."

He led me into a small restaurant and bought two bowls of *thentuk*.[101] While he was having his soup, he took out a bottle of *chang* from a yellow bag and drank from it in big gulps. Suspecting that he would get drunk, I advised him to drink only a little. However, he explained to me at length that he didn't get intoxicated from *chang*. In front of my eyes the bottle was half emptied and I had no choice but to force him to stop. Finally, listening to my words, he stopped drinking and we started on our way towards Siling.

It became completely dark. In the celestial sphere the clear white full moon was smiling and showing its row of white teeth. The rabbit in the middle of the moon[102] was sleeping its peaceful, contented sleep, and the constellations of stars were resting, smiling in their own abodes. Who could have known that on this night, when the sky was so clear and the moon shining so brightly, there would be sudden harm caused by an evil eclipse?

That person who was behaving in an affectionate and familiar manner towards me was actually a wolf in the guise of a sheep, a fox full of deceit. He was pretending to be drunk and embraced me, holding my shoulders. Acting as if he was staggering, he pushed me to the ground and I understood that something terrible would happen. With all my might I tried to free myself, but in vain. Then the wicked and cruel rain of mud soiled the stainless petals of the flower of my youth, tingeing them with dirt. Though I regret it, it was too late. Now there was no way I could go to Tshering and also I couldn't hold up my head among others of the same age. Again and again I thought that it would be better to die than live like this. As there was no way of suppressing the suffering in my mind, I cried out loudly. From the direction I was facing at that time, I saw the dark shadow of a human being approaching under the moonlight and I also heard the sound of hasty steps running away. Before my eyes arose a whirl of reddish fireflies and my ears were pounding. Then it turned dark inside my head and I lost consciousness.

When I recovered, the light of the early morning had spread over the expanse of the panorama, making it shining and bright. A cold brisk wind was blowing, stirring the nearby grasses and bushes. I was lying by the side of a small ravine and my body had been covered with a sheet of white felt. Feeling slightly astonished, I lifted my head. There was a nun squatting by my side and she was looking at me with a smile. She asked, "Didn't you feel cold last night?"

I shook my head replying, "I wasn't cold. Not at all. Where have you come from?" I asked her. The nun looked at me with an expression of infinite sympathy and said, "Get up now! Are you on your way to Siling? Let's go together and talk."

She had come from Labrang to Kumbum on pilgrimage. On our way she asked me a lot of questions and I told her my story exactly as it had happened. She said: "Only the Three Jewels[103] know. You are really a girl of bad *karma*!"

After we had arrived at Siling, she said to me, "Lhakyi, according to what you've told me, Tshering seems to be a kind and conscientious person. Though it's commonly believed that an undesirable, bad thing has happened to you, if you tell him honestly how it happened he won't blame you for it. In my opinion it's best for you to go to Tongkhor."

"No." Now that I had become a defiled girl, how could I go to Tshering? Even if Tshering didn't scold me, could he tolerate me in his mind? Even if he could tolerate me could he trust me later? Goodness! What an unfortunate girl I am. My connection with him was now completely finished. As I didn't have the confidence to go to meet Tshering, I shook my head.

"Then, where do you plan to go now?"

Where should I go? There was nowhere to go. The Lord of Death was waiting for me. Except for a hell-realm there was nowhere to go. I again shook my head as before and couldn't utter a single word in answer.

"Then for the meantime let's go together to Labrang. Later we'll find some solution and make plans. If you don't have any other idea, we shall start on our way tomorrow."

Next day before sunrise I started towards Labrang with her. The sun appeared, smiling from behind the eastern mountain tops after laying the red and yellow ornaments of morning clouds on the neck of the girl of dawn. The sky was blue and clear resembling an unblemished huge flat jewel which has just been bathed in water. The long, slow-moving Tsongchu river of Siling was still asleep under its cover of ice and once in a while drew a light, snoring breath. On the macadamed highway a few buses honking their horns as they drove east. I walked the highway beside the long course of the Tsongchu river with heavy steps and, while following Nun Dölma, the following big questions arose, one by one, on the surface of the mirror of my pure mind: Do parents who speak about a girl's marriage publicly, while she's still in her mother's womb, have any shame? Though one's physical form is created by one's parents, is it a Tibetan custom that one doesn't have any control over one's own body? Oh, what did it mean that the flower of love, which emerged from the union of affectionate thoughts between Tshering and me, was destroyed like this by frost and that the petals of the flower of my youth—of a girl desiring worldly life and future happiness—were suddenly withered? Did all this happen because of the momentum of my past actions ...?

Dölma's Empathy

Dear friends, learned readers, if you have taken a look at the above accounts, you may, like me, a nun, feel sympathy for the main character of the story, Lhakyi and wish to know what kind of changes relating to these events took place in Lhakyi's life after her arrival at Labrang. I, a nun, got my body stuck in a place where even my head wouldn't fit,[104] and the end of this story is perhaps also something you cannot imagine. However, due to the force of shared actions and a life of solitude, Lhakyi's and my thoughts became harmonious like water and milk blended together. During the period when we experienced the hardships of solitude, Lhakyi and I, like a body and its shadow, didn't separate from each other. The happenings after Lhakyi arrived at Labrang are clear to me and I shall relate them.

My name is Dölma Pelmo and I am fifty-five years old. When thinking over my life as a nun it has sometimes been ridiculous, a few times tearful and sometimes depressing. I am not at all clear about what the happiness of a human life means. Since my childhood a Mount Meru of suffering has piled up in my innocent, pure mind and an ocean of suffering has whirled between my lungs and liver.

Both my parents died when I was small and therefore I had no choice but to get married when I was fifteen years old. "The friend for my whole life", whose mouth was silkier than milk and insides sharper than a thorn, was an old man twice my age whose face was all covered with ugly wrinkles. I was only nominally his wife, but actually a servant to him and his sisters. The sufferings of the noble Milarepa, his mother and sister, descended upon me and the way I suffered was even twice as much as Nyangtsha Kargyen.[105] However, who can erase the lines of fate inscribed on one's forehead as a result of what one has done in one's previous life? Not long after that my "husband" died. At that time I was already more than four months pregnant, against my wishes. Despite that his sister, like a demoness with iron lips and nails, grabbed my hair and dragged me to the door. She pierced my eardrums with the sharp spear of harsh words, calling me a destroyer and a prostitute, and after she had thoroughly abused me I wandered on the roads like a stray dog. I didn't have a single relative close to me except the dark shadow accompanying me and my pale knees as my bedmate. Though I gave birth to a baby girl in the mid-winter of that year, her clothes were poor and there was no food so this child who was like a part of my heart died from hunger and cold. During this very life I actually experienced what is called the suffering of hell after death. At that time I was still under twenty years old.

Then, while begging, I went to the grasslands of Gengya[106] and asked for a place to stay with a nomad family. The mistress of the family asked me many questions and I answered them honestly. She said: "Then, girl, you can be the wife of my son."

Although she and her son weren't well-off, since they were affectionate and compassionate towards me I started to live a happy life. But how could a woman of bad *karma* like me have the good luck to be happy? After two or three months my only loved one, to whom I'd entrusted all the longings of my love, was forcibly taken to join warlord Ma's bandits and dragged away.[107] Even though we had been married for only a short time, we had great affection for each other. Because of that, he escaped from the army and then, unfortunately, became the target of a bullet from a bearded general under Ma. As her only son had died, my old mother-in-law also passed away from anguish. Then I buried the corpses of these people who had been kind to me, and to create positive potential for both of them and to acquire good merit for myself, I bowed my head at the feet of a proper lama and took the vows of a layperson.[108]

Oh, readers, has this bored you? Really, you're not to be blamed for that. I became lost in narrating my own story of misery and forgot to write Lhakyi's story. The speech of a senile nun doesn't have any deep meaning. Now I shall leave it aside. I'll again take a clean sheet of paper and narrate the story of Lhakyi from the beginning.

Lhakyi—A blighted flower! You are also a girl with bad *karma*. But what else could we have in common? I am an animal of the old society who knows how to speak like a human. You are a young girl of the new society who has control over her own body. I am an orphan of the old society whereas you are a beloved child of the new society having both parents. I... You...

Every time Lhakyi told me of her desire to become a nun, my mind became disturbed and I was forced to compare in detail the old and new societies and Lhakyi and me. Never mind having a good period like this before, even if there'd been only a small fraction of it I wouldn't have wanted to become a nun. Especially as Lhakyi is still young, and on top of being a good-looking girl she also has a nice boyfriend called Tshering, I thought that if Lhakyi became ordained instead of it being a virtue it would be the very opposite. I would commit the sin of separating a husband and wife. What Lhakyi has said is true. There is nothing more shameful and sad than a young girl, who has not yet enjoyed the warmth of being together with a young boy whom she loves, being abused by another bad person. Each time when I see Lhakyi's long, dark, thick shining braids, her smiling youthful face with its red and white complexion and the thin, long and flexible shape of her body, I feel overwhelming sympathy for her. Thinking her talk of becoming a nun was like a young boy's boastful speech or a young girl's deceptive words, I didn't take it seriously.

Now two whole months have passed since we first met on the road to Kumbum and then arrived at Labrang. During those days and nights we opened our hearts to each other and hid nothing.[109] Judging from her words and expressions it seems that my judgement was close to the truth. Her talk of becoming a nun is talk from the top of the throat.[110] Her longing for Tshering was the secret in the depths of her mind.

Therefore I told her in many different ways[111] about the happiness of family life in the new society, how the appearance of young boys and girls is softer than white wool, the love of parents and children is deeper than the blue waters of a lake, and how arguments and unhappiness are like bubbles in water. Lhakyi bent her head and didn't say anything. After that, although she still requested me a few times to let her become a nun, I said to her, "There is no great benefit for the Doctrine in merely looking like an ordained person. Better than that is to have unwavering faith in the Three Jewels and to recite some *mani*-mantras which will be of benefit in future lives. Basically, getting rid of wrong-doing depends mainly on your own mind, and even if you don't have the appearance of an ordained person if there's faith in your mind there is no fault. That is most important."

The three winter months passed at their own pace and the signs of the three spring months appeared almost unnoticed before our eyes. This is the best season for staying in solitude, and therefore Lhakyi and I went to Thrating of Lhe in Gengye Tingring, which is the birthplace of The All-Knowing Jamyang Zhedpa Ngawang Tsöndrü.[112] At that time I met two pilgrims from Lhakyi's homeland and, as I thought that her parents were certainly worried, I sent a clear message informing them that Lhakyi was with me and urging them to come to fetch her soon. But for a while I had to keep these things secret from Lhakyi.

On the grassy plain of Gengya the signs of the arrival of spring's glory are not that evident and the peaks of the distant mountains were still wrapped in the white snow which doesn't melt even during summer, in the sixth month of the year. Although the grass still seems pale, if you look carefully, you can see the slender spikes of green shoots in the midst of the pale clumps. Since the marvellous sun is shining in the clear blue sky, spreading its tender warmth, it's certain that the glory of spring will soon arrive on the grasslands of Gengya.

Lhakyi and I went on our way after we'd been given provisions by some patrons in Gengya. All the nomad families in that area gave us plenty of meat, butter, cheese, toasted barley flour and other things. In the beginning, while I was begging Lhakyi's face blushed completely red and, especially if there were some young men in the house and we met them, like the leaves on a willow branch she hung her head and was unable to raise it.

"If you and Tshering would get together again, I could get a patron free from avarice."

I spoke like that to Lhakyi, making my words sound deeply meaningful, while we were walking along in the snow carrying our provisions.

"What is the meaning of 'a patron'?" she asked uncertainly.

"Oh, patron? For example, after you have gone back to your homeland and married Tshering, if both of you give me some provisions so that I can lead a religious life and practice virtue, you and Tshering will be my patrons and I your spiritual guide."

"If one becomes a nun, does one have to be a beggar all one's life?"

"You fool, you would die of starvation if you didn't beg."

"I'm sure it's good to become a nun, but this need to beg..."

Generally, there are several ways to explain about begging, but, since from the start I didn't like the idea of Lhakyi becoming a nun, the moment her mind had entered this web of doubt I explained how her becoming a nun would be an act of despair and hopelessness and how this would make it difficult to repay the kindness of her elders and her beloved life companion. If you, Lhakyi, disappoint the hopes of your beloved friend and your kind parents, becoming a nun would not be a virtuous deed; not only that, it would be gathering sins and negative actions. When I told her such things she nodded her head, as if she had understood, and said, "Then it's also all right if I don't become a nun. But I definitely won't return to my homeland. You are old, and it will be comfortable if you have somebody like me serving you, so I'll stay with you until your death."

"You fool, that would be a great mistake. Now, while you are healthy and able to enjoy all the good things in life, what would be the point of not enjoying them and accompanying a nun like me?"

I jokingly told her episodes from that time in my youth when I'd lived with my husband, creating exaggerations, and she blushed and told me many secret words that had been exchanged between her and Tshering.

"Oh, it is really so. Indeed, how pleasant those things are!"

As I said these things her face turned very red and, seeing the look of hesitation in her eyes, it seemed that her thoughts were clearly revealed. However, her head was shaking like a prayer flag inscribed with *mani-*

mantras fluttering in the wind. Looking at that, it seemed as if she was trying to hide the very obvious expression on her face.

"If your father comes to fetch you, will you go back with him?"

"No, I won't. I won't go at all. He's not my father. I don't have anybody who can be called 'a father'. I don't even need one."

Lhakyi's words were beyond my comprehension and listening to her tone it sounded like the roaring of a wild beast. She gave the impression that her father was actually a demon.

"Then, if Tshering came to fetch you...?"

Lhakyi shook her head as it were a *damaruḥ*.[113]

"It isn't possible that he would come. He won't come."

She repeated that in a low and weak tone of voice. Finally, heaving a long sigh, a flow of tears burst from her eyes.

"If Tshering were to come..." While I purposely said this, Lhakyi shook her head as before and didn't utter a single word.

As Lhakyi was not used to living in the midst of snow and in solitude she developed a revulsion towards it. Her two small eyes which had been smiling before like drops of water and had laughed like youthful flowers, sank in their sockets and her eyes bulged. Her two cheeks which had resembled apples also turned pale and swelled. Her braids turned into a big town for the festivities of lice and their young.

Around that time, Lhakyi's father arrived. Though I thought to myself that now the time for Lhakyi's wishes to be fulfilled had come, the result of the meeting of the father and his daughter was beyond my imagination. Lhakyi's father was a big man. He had dark skin and among the wrinkles on his forehead one could see the expression of a stubborn person.

"You shameless wanderer woman. Go, go!"

The way he threatened Lhakyi immediately on seeing her was similar to the situation of a slave in the old society falling into the hands of his owner.

"I won't go. I won't go at all," Lhakyi said with the fire of anger flaming in her eyes.

If this continued everything would surely turn upside down. So I quickly approached them and said to Lhakyi's father, "Don't be angry. If you have something to say, say it peacefully. Lhakyi will surely listen to you."

He pushed me away and said, "You old nun who has taught my daughter all kinds of evil things, don't stick your body into a place where your head wouldn't fit. Put your finger to your mouth and stay silent."

Lhakyi took out her knife and cut through one of her thick braids, throwing it in front of her father. She took hold of the other braid. When she was holding the knife and was about to cut that braid too, I rushed to prevent her. But before I could reach her that braid had also fallen to the ground.

At once, Lhakyi's father ran forward like a madman and kneeled down on the floor. Beating his chest with his fists he appealed to her repeatedly, "My dear daughter, don't do that. Listen to your father and let's return home."

The wind blew, tousling the hair on Lhakyi's head and she stood there majestically like a lion showing off its blue mane.[114] It was not clear whether she was angry or actually tossing her blue mane. However, both her legs were trembling and her whole body was shaking as if all the beings on earth were being jolted by an earthquake.

Lhakyi's father waited for a few days. I also did my best to appeal to Lhakyi and give her some advice. However, the young girl was as lofty as the top of Mount Meru and our efforts turned out to be fruitless. How true is the saying that "the beauty of a horse is spoiled if its body is too small and the beauty of a man is spoiled if he is short tempered." Although both the father and his daughter had now sunk into an ocean of regret, they couldn't humble themselves in front of each other until the waves of their anger had subsided. After I had told Lhakyi's father a lot of things, such as that he should go back for a while and afterwards, if they sent Tshering to fetch her, Lhakyi would surely return, Lhakyi's father said, "I entrust the happiness and sorrows of my daughter to you. Tshering is also about to return from Tongkhor. When the summer comes I will send him here," and he left for home.

When he was about to depart, I placed the two thick braids of Lhakyi's hair in his hands and said, "These are not ordinary braids of hair, but witnesses to the story of a young girl growing up. Inside these braids lie the kindness of the parents, the happiness of childhood and the delights of a new way of life. Moreover, especially therein lies the love of a young man and the wishes of a young girl attached to a life yet to come. Therefore, that you caused Lhakyi to cut them off is not a leaf of suffering but the root of happiness. Lhakyi is a person suffering from negative *karma*. I place all my hopes in Tshering and have written in this letter all that has happened to Lhakyi. If he has any morality and compassion, my hopes won't turn out to be empty. Here, give this letter and the braids to Tshering."

So saying, I gave him the letter which I had written with great effort during the whole day and night.

Lhakyi's father returned to his homeland. Since Lhakyi was again urging me to give her the nun's vow, I acted as if I was giving her the vow and taught her the Confession of Downfalls, Refuge and the Praises to White and Green Tārā. I tried to console her and she, not realising that I had deceived her, said with great joy, "Now I am a pure *upāsikā* who has entered into the world of Buddha's teachings."

One day she said to me, "Doesn't my hair have to be shaved off?" I again gave her various false explanations about the rules of *upāsikā*, telling her that although it was allowed to shave one's head, one was also permitted not to do so. I was not making her shave off her hair. Only the Three Jewels know. Right at this moment I confess all those negativities accumulated by lies and deceits that were concocted in order to restore the happiness of a young innocent girl. Please hear me.

The glory of the three summer months arrived. The earth was green and the flowers beautiful. In the summer season, which gives fresh energy to all creatures, the sweet song of the cuckoo sounds in the distance, the insects and bees hum melodiously on the grassy plain and in the forests the *jölmo*[115] displays the agility of its wings. The glory of the summer will certainly also arise in Lhakyi's mind. Tshering, at this time when the splendour of the three summer months and the cuckoo have come, why have you not yet arrived?

Phüntshog's Realisation

After I returned from the hermitage of Gengya, near Labrang Tashi Khyil, many thoughts were revolving in my mind. Wangtsho's lamentations and Lhakyi's braids were like mournful music haunting me. The past events came to my mind like images being screened from a film and Wangtsho's voice saying in her sleep, "Bring back my girl.

Bring back my girl" as well as Lhakyi's firm replies such as "I won't go. I definitely won't go", were echoing in my ears and wouldn't fade away. Even during the time of the old society I hadn't experienced anything so exasperating and desperate. I hadn't been so afraid even when the brigands tied me up and were about to run me through with their swords.

Oh dear! Now ... now, what has happened to me? My legs are trembling and in front of my eyes there are constant small flashes flaming like sparks. I can't rely on myself and don't have control over my own mind. Lhakyi! Ah, Lhakyi! You are a part of my own flesh and blood. Do you know how happy I felt from the day your mother Wangtsho conceived? For your sake, when I had a mouthful of delicious food I couldn't bring myself to eat it. When I had half a metre of good cloth I couldn't wear it. Oh, although in this world innumerable parents are loving to their children, there are only a few children who understand the kindness of their parents. Though I, your father, cannot lead you up to the heavens, how would I dare to send you down to the hells?

How happy Lhamo and Rigyag are now! It's a Tibetan custom that the parents decide on their children's marriage. Because of my past actions, I had to plead with my own daughter. Wise people say this is a degenerate age. Does that mean that during this degenerate age the roles of father and daughter are reversed? What the old Tibetan proverb says is really true, "A girl cannot bear happiness. An ass cannot bear a golden saddle." And as another proverb says, "A person who does not know how to make the most of the joy he has will complain of pains in his bottom when mounted on the most excellent horse." For that reason she is wandering around over passes and through different places like a stray dog, begging for food like a beggar. Now she is friends with a nun, and has rebelled against her father. It will be a misfortune for me and the party, and people of our area will make up rumours criticising her parents. It's true that even though girls have long hair, their minds are short. So, as soon as I saw Lhakyi's expression, instead of feeling compassion I got angry and threatened her.

But it was beyond my imagination that she would take a knife and cut her hair. Honestly speaking, I lost my bravery and courage. As Lhakyi is my older daughter, if she becomes a nun...

Oh, dear! I don't want to think about these things and don't dare to either. An invisible force entered me stealthily and silently and created a bitter-sweet flavour in my mind. It caused me to sink into an uneasiness that was difficult to bear. Looking at Wangtsho I felt compassion for her, and when I remembered Lhakyi's behaviour I got angry. What could cause Lhakyi to harbour such a grudge and hatred towards me? Why did Rigyag and Lhamo suddenly get married? What a deep secret all these matters are! Even if I go to Nyima, my blood brother, to talk it over with him, he is, like me, a deceived stranger blind in the fog. Doubtless Rigyag and Lhamo understand what caused this. However, to try to get words from their mouths is as hopeless as looking for ivory in a dog's mouth and would be a fruitless task. Moreover, they are still turning the stones of hints and throwing the arrows of curses, saying, "Old man Phüntshog, don't act senile before you get senile. If you have the mouth of a tiger for eating, you need to have the stomach of a vulture for digestion. You know these matters very clearly."

"Have I actually caused these things to happen?"

I turned on my back in bed and talking to myself I reflected for a long time.[116] But I couldn't see at all how I could have brought about those events.

"If you haven't caused them, who has done it?", Wangtsho said to me in tears.

"Oh, tell me straight. Where is the proof that I've caused them?"

Between loud sobs Wangtsho said, "The man that Lhakyi wants and who is her beloved... is Tshering. You... What is the reason that you... forcibly gave her to Rigyag? ... Do you know... the suffering that girl has gone through? Yah, you old ghost! Old ghost! Go and bring my daughter here..."[117]

"As a father, do I not even have the right to give my daughter in marriage?"

"You dog, keep your mouth closed! Is my daughter an animal? If an animal doesn't want to go somewhere, haven't you seen it stalling?"

"Anyway, that is an ancient Tibetan proverb. It is the custom and tradition of the snowy land of Tibet."

"Whenever you open your mouth it's a proverb, and when you close it it's a tradition. When a child is in its mother's womb, and no one knows whether it's a boy or a girl, is it a Tibetan proverb to discuss its marriage? Is sending a girl to her death a Tibetan tradition? You are creating a proverb where there's none. Is it permitted to introduce a tradition where there is none? Your proverbs are bad omens. Those traditions are hurtful traditions."

Truly. If it's put like that, I can't give any reasons. What does it mean when a good action brings forth this kind of bad result? Does the law of *karma* exist or not? If it exists, why has a double load of suffering fallen on my head? For whole nights I'm unable to sleep and I don't even want to. When I think it over there's truth in what Wangtsho says. However, there's no way to discipline these modern girls. Is that due to the pride of the young girls or to the helplessness of the parents? Or... oh! It is so! It is so! In the Tibetan radio programme, when they were explaining about the marriage law, they spoke out against parents forcing their daughters to marry. Tashi, the secretary of the commune, said, "Old man, You'll surely make mistakes when you look at new matters with an old brain."

Those are solely political matters, and because I'm totally illiterate and do not thoroughly understand those policies and because I am not aware of recent developments perhaps I have caused this myself. These days one can hear the young boys of the village saying that if a father forces a girl to marry she will commit suicide. Luckily such a disaster hasn't befallen me. Oh, dear! If Lhakyi had taken that course it would all be my fault. Though I wouldn't be beheaded, I would surely be imprisoned. If an old man like me were imprisoned, on the verge of old age and death, it would bring doom to that life.

I fell asleep in a state of fear. Although I had various nightmares I couldn't interpret them clearly.

"Hey! Get up! Tshering has come back! Hey! Get up immediately! Tshering has come back!"

A distant voice echoed in my ears and rolling over on my side I awoke. Rubbing my eyes, I looked up and saw Wangtsho standing beside me with an expression of suffering on her face.

"Aa...?" I asked, not knowing what was the matter.

Wangtsho gestured with her lips to the right, and said: "Old man! Get up immediately! Tshering has returned."[118]

I rolled over and got up. Without even washing myself I rushed to the house of my blood brother Nyima.

Tshering's Thoughts

I completed my studies successfully at the school in Tongkhor. As I was returning home by bus from Siling the glory of summer had appeared on the earth and the flowers of joy were smiling abundantly in my mind as well. Were both my parents well? Had my elder brother Rigyag found a girlfriend? Lhakyi—my girlfriend, whom I'd missed day and night—was probably waiting for me as though starving for food or thirsty for water. Perhaps she had missed me so much that even her face had become gaunt. I was staring out from the window of the bus on the highway leading towards my home and various images arose in my mind. I had bought a flower-patterned blouse, leather shoes and some other presents for Lhakyi from Siling. Taking them out from my black bag, I glanced at them repeatedly. I thought that when Lhakyi wore these shoes she would surely be even more beautiful than before and one wouldn't be able to stop looking at her.

However, when I stepped over the threshold of our house I felt slightly uneasy. The reason for that was that though my father saw me coming, he acted as though he hadn't seen me and went further into the house.

"Father!" I called out to him. He turned his head from the inner door of the house and looked at me carefully. Then he came to me and said, "Tshering. Is it... is it you?" Father's voice was trembling and weak, and he didn't dare look at me. Moreover, if my eyes weren't mistaken, even his legs were shaking badly.

"Father. Are you feeling all right? Aren't you suffering from some sickness or fever?"

"No. No. I'm ... fine. Yah, how nice this is, nice indeed. Come in."

It was almost dusk, but as no butterlamps had been lit it was very dark inside the house and I couldn't see anything. The fire in the stove was embers and I couldn't hear anything except my mother's voice welcoming me. Though Rigyag took the bag from my hands, I still didn't recognise him. At that moment it became light inside the house and at the same time I saw a new woman in the light of the butterlamp. Both my parents and my elder brother were standing near me and that new woman was Lhamo.

"Are all of you fine?" I asked in greeting.

"We are fine, we are all fine. Where have you come from?" said the voice of my elder brother.

"Today I've come from Siling."

"Yah, daughter-in-law, make some tea quickly." Immediately, when my father said that, I understood that Lhamo was the daughter-in-law of our family. She came back carrying firewood and stoked the fire. Pouring water from a pan on the stove into a copper pot, she placed it over the fire. In the light of the butterlamp, and from the fire in the stove, I could see that all the family had different expressions on their faces and were looking stealthily at me. None of them spoke to me.

My father was staring at the copper pot on the stove, mother was reciting *mani*-mantras, my elder brother was continuously scratching his head and sister-in-law was reaching her hand towards the flames of the fire.

"Goodness! What has happened to all of you?" I said and "In case none of you likes me, I can go to the commune after staying overnight. However, you must tell me precisely why you don't like me."

"Tshering," father said in a slightly irritated manner, "Won't you let us make some tea? Now that you are a government employee, are you using your power over both your parents?"

"Then, you...?"

"Tshering. Mother's darling. As you've come from faraway Siling today you must be feeling hungry. When the tea has boiled, first eat and quench your thirst and after that we'll talk."

Mother interrupted my words in this way and I became even more suspicious than before.

I had no choice but to wait for a while. With a false smile I stared at the copper pot on the stove.

After I'd drunk my tea the tiredness gradually vanished. Sister-in-law asked me about matters related to my studies in Tongkhor and about what good merchandise was available in Siling. I replied precisely to her questions. After that, father discussed the marriage of Lhamo and Rigyag. According to him, Lhamo and Rigyag had settled the matter themselves. Moreover, since both sets of parents had already had thoughts of that sort, they had married on the fifteenth day of Losar of the previous year. Since it was said that my father had never lied in his life, and since all the people of the village trusted his word, I thought that what he said was the truth.

However, it was not until I lay down beside my elder brother Rigyag in that wooden hut as we'd done before, that I understood what a big lie my father had told. As my older brother was an honest person, he told me exactly about those events of which I was unaware: about Lhakyi's father's and my father's secret discussion, about Lhamo's deceit, about his own illusions, and Lhakyi's suffering... Oh dear! All those events were such that I couldn't even have dreamt about them.

"I swore not to speak to anybody about this. But to show the sincere love that Lhakyi has for you, I have to break my vow."

While my older brother Rigyag was explaining about the relationship between him and Lhakyi, he also related in detail how father had stubbornly ordered them to go to fetch a marriage certificate and how Lhakyi had tried to commit suicide.

"Tshering, honestly speaking you've been almost too secretive. If you had only told me about the relationship between you and Lhakyi before; was it really necessary for things to reach this point? Lhakyi almost..."

Listening to my older brother's words, Lhakyi's face gaunt with suffering, her voice crying out in despair, how she had put a belt round her neck when all other ways had failed, how she had shaken when her breath was blocked and so on, all of this was as if I were actually seeing it before my own eyes and really hearing it with my own ears. I felt immeasurable sympathy for her and, recollecting the many kinds of suffering she had experienced for my sake, I felt overwhelming distress and was so desperate that tears streamed from my eyes.

"Then why, instead of coming to see me, did Lhakyi go to Labrang?" I asked my elder brother, because I didn't understand clearly.

"I see. I've also thought about that many times, but I couldn't find a logical answer. Probably..."

"Yah, say it!" When I saw my older brother hesitating I urged him to speak out.

"In my opinion, she probably met some ruffian from Labrang on the road and he did something shameful to her."

"What?" My older brother's words split both my lungs and heart like a meteorite striking a rocky mountain or like a country divided by a flood; it was as if my lungs and liver were upside down. Lhakyi! Ah, Lhakyi! Have you really changed your mind? Or is it possible that a rough and sharp poisonous thorn like a sword of deceit has made its way under the skin of your charming face, beautiful as a flower? It's not possible. It can't be like that. But why have you wandered to the ends of the world? Where are you now...?

My mind was pondering many thoughts, and then it started to get light. My elder brother's snoring and the crowing of the cock entered my ears simultaneously.

"Tshering!"

I heard the voice of an old man I knew. I didn't need to think who it was. It was Lhakyi's father, Phüntshog.

Since I didn't reply, the door of the wooden hut where I was sleeping opened with a creaking sound and at once my older brother and I got up, one after the other, and sat on our beds. The sun had already risen. With tears in his eyes Phüntshog said, "Tshering, dear. If you can't help now, I, an old man, will be imprisoned in my old age. Look here! That demoness!", and he showed me two long braids of hair that were dark, thick and shiny.

When I looked carefully at those two braids they were of slightly different lengths and by the look of it they seemed to have been hacked off just a bit more than a finger's length from the nape of her neck.

"Aren't these Lhakyi's braids?" I asked in alarm.

"Yes, they are. They are the braids of that demoness." Phüntshog was getting angry.

Phüntshog was a stubborn man, and probably because Lhakyi hadn't listened to him he had got furious and chopped off her braids. At that moment the things that my older brother had told me came uncontrollably into my mind, and because both suffering and anger arose simultaneously it became unbearable.

"Why did you cut her braids?"

"No, Tshering, I didn't cut these braids."

"Then who did?"

"That... that demoness. Look, why should anybody abuse me like this? I do have faults, but, these braids..." When I heard this, my heart was pumping powerfully and I felt like fainting.

"I thought of doing something good for Lhakyi, but she herself..."

"Treating your own daughter like a beggar and making her wander everywhere—it's hardly being good to her. It is really true that Mr Wolf eats the delicious meat and the blame is borne by Ms Fox. What good does it do to deny one's own faults which are like a mountain and discuss the faults of others which are like a flea? If you are not to be blamed, Lhakyi is not to be criticised either."

"It's true. It's true. Now you've understood. There's nothing I can do about it."

Phüntshog was shaking his head and he told me about the events which took place on his trip to Labrang, one by one. After that he took a letter from his pouch and gave it to me. "Here is a letter," he said.

I took the letter, unfolded it and looked at it. It contained the few words written below:

To the considerate and open-minded young man Tshering,

I am a nun and my name is Dölma. Due to the suffering and abuse Lhakyi has suffered for your sake, the flower of her youth is almost blighted by frost and snow and the petals of love directed towards you are also about to close. However, she has no one else to trust and no one in whom she can place her hopes throughout her days and nights but you alone. If you have a little concern for her, come without delay to fetch Lhakyi. All her joys and sorrows depend on you; please keep that in your mind. It is not easy to write everything in detail here, but I will tell it all to you when we meet. Dated.

Now there was nothing to wait for. I quickly got up from my bed and went to the commune. After having reported about my studies, I requested leave for fifteen days and set out to fetch Lhakyi.

Everything that had happened drifted away behind me, like the flow of a river. I saw before my eyes a great and wide highway and smelled the fragrance of flowers. In a distant forest a cuckoo was singing its melodious song.

When the cuckoo comes from Mön
It marks the beginning of spring
When it arrives among the trees
The glory of summer is smiling.

Truly, when you, the messenger of spring, arrive at my homeland, summer has come. Even though you arrive slightly late, how melodious your sweet voice is...

A Shameless Bride

❖

Döndrub Gyel and Tshering Döndrub

One

High mountains, low earth, serpentine water-streams, dense forests and the rest—everything in this world was enveloped by a veil of fog. Grey, secluded, silent. If this curtain of fog had not been there, the scene would have been as beautiful and attractive as a drawing by an artist or a well-written poem. However, because the whole earth was enveloped by fog today, the glory of the smiling flowers of the summer months, the dance of the birds showing the skill of their wings and the melodious humming of bees—these good features had turned into secret hidden qualities. The serpentine path leading to Dragkar Sermojong was also covered by fog and had vanished from sight. Oh, what could be that dark shadow there on that small path? Could it be a bear or maybe a yeti? In this plain of thick forests there are certainly many wild animals. However, judging by its way of moving that shadowy shape was not an animal but a two-legged creature walking erect.

In fact it was an old lame man who had passed beyond his youth. He was wearing an old worn out four-cornered hat[119] on his head. It was thick with grease and as an ornament on his neck marked by wrinkles he was wearing a rosary of red sandal-wood beads. From the way he was carrying a long square rucksack placed sideways on his back, he seemed like a yogic practitioner wandering from one hermitage to the other, but he kept wiping the sweat away from his forehead wrinkled with suffering and repeated the words "In this world of cyclic existence there is no happiness even that of the size of a mustard seed." This showed that he was a lay house-holder. As the old man was lame, his steps were uneven and his left and right shoulders were also not level. The way he walked holding a crooked stick of white willow-wood in his hand for support was like the jumping of a wounded musk-deer in the middle of a forest.

"Phew...!" The old lame man heaved a sigh. It seemed that he was tired. Resting his stick under his armpit, he sat down on a big stone by the way-side and as he wiped the sweat away from his forehead with his sleeve, a long sigh escaped from his lips.

"Fa...ther... ...!"

Suddenly, from the thick forested valley covered with fog, a girl's clear voice rang out. Like the thundering voice of the blue turquoise dragon breaking through the cover of dark clouds, it immediately demolished the silent solitude of the sleeping forest. That goddess of sound—the echo—prolonged the sound causing it to travel through passes and valleys.

"Ah!... Sang...mo... I am here..." As soon as that lame man heard the voice, he got frightened and disturbed like a wounded wild animal who has heard the sound of a gun. "What a curse this leg is ...", and he beat with his fists on his left leg. Then, hastily, leaning on his stick, he started on the narrow mountain path and moving forward, his steps were like the gait of a musk-deer with a broken leg making its way in the forest.

Two

Actually, that old lame man is called Zöpa, one of the people living near Labrang, and that young girl is Zöpa's daughter Küntu Sangmo. Zöpa's leg was injured over ten years ago when the Red Guards descended on the heads of all living creatures. Although he had later consulted a doctor and undergone all possible treatments like taking medicine and the application of moxibustion, nothing had helped. And so they were on their way to the hot-springs of Dragkar, the daughter leading her father.

"Ghost ... ghost! Look at your way of walking! Come quickly!" The beautiful and young Küntu Sangmo commanded her father with her hands on her hips.

"Ya, ya, ya, Sangmo, I am coming as fast as I can but this curse of mine... ..." said Zöpa in a weak voice, touching his left leg.

"That is purely your own loss. Who has made you carry legs like that? Go on, go on! Don't make excuses."

"Ya, ya, ya, I'm coming, I'm coming."

The girl's words jagged his memory. On the screen of Zöpa's snow-white mind, the mind of an old-man who had experienced much suffering, the sad events of the past arose vividly like the pictures of a movie.

Oh, that was an event which had taken place in the fifties. Zöpa had been an ordained monk with maroon robes. However, due to the time and many other conditions, he had disrobed, got married with a woman from nearby Labrang and had started to enjoy the happiness of worldly life. After one year, a daughter was born and she was given the name Küntu Sangmo. When she reached nine years of age, a great famine spread everywhere in that region and her mother died of starvation. From then on Zöpa became the substitute for both the parents and he took affectionate care of his daughter born from his own flesh and blood who was like the eyes in his head and like his heart. During the course of time, Küntu Sangmo gradually grew up and her mental faculties and intelligence became clever and sharp. Zöpa was immeasurably happy at having such a clever and intelligent daughter and when Küntu Sangmo arrived home carrying water, swept the house with a broom, prepared food in a cooking pot, offered her father tea and soup holding the bowl between her soft long white flexible hands, and when she was engaged in other tasks, who could have described the happiness and joy that Zöpa felt? However, just as the bees circle where there are flowers, so even though Sangmo was young, since she was good looking, she became a topic of discussion between the young men of her own and other villages and some suitors appeared asking to marry her. Among them was Jili Lhündrub from the outskirts of Labrang who was said to be his father's heir. He sent his father with a flask of beer and a greeting scarf two or three times to their doorstep. Moreover the girl herself was willing to get married, but how could old Zöpa bear to give away his daughter?

How true is the saying "Happiness is impermanent like the dewdrops on the blades of grass." During the times when fear of the Red Guards descended upon the heads of all living beings, Zöpa turned into an enemy of the people and a target for the progressives with red labels on their arms.

"What serious fault do I have? I'm actually just an ordinary monk from a monastery... ..."

Every time Zöpa had to undergo a struggle-session at the hands of the progressives, he silently reflected in this way.

"Zöpa, the wolf among the sheep! The weed in the field! The enemy of the people, if you confess your faults, we will be lenient. If you do not admit them, we will use violence." That was the voice of that wicked Silin Lhündrub.[120]

"All right, all right, but I... ..."

"Ts... ts...! You enemy of the people! In 1958 when you took part in the fighting, how many soldiers of the People's Liberation Army did you kill? Count them immediately!"

"Enemy, count!"

"Count immediately!"

"I did not take part in the fighting. After this area was liberated in 1950, I disrobed. After that, though I did some recitations, I did not have any relations with the monastery. During the fighting, I even showed the way to the PLA. Those facts are well-known to everybody."

"Do not lie! Then why do we not know about it?"

"At that time you were still very young... ..."

"If you confess your faults, we will be lenient, and if you do not admit them, we will use force."

The final words for ending the session filled the assembly hall. When Zöpa was returning home, he felt tired and as if the energy in his body was spent. The struggle session was carried on like that for a few days, but the progressives did not obtain any results. After some days, a meeting was called again to struggle with Zöpa.

That wicked Silin Lhündrub, looking haughty, asked Zöpa to tell about his crime of hiding a gun.

"Since my birth, I have never held a gun in my hand."

With all his force, Zöpa declared his innocence.

At that moment, a young girl came up to Zöpa and pointed her finger at his forehead. She said, "Zöpa, you enemy! Did you not hide that gun which is beside our cupboard?", said his daughter Küntu Sangmo, who had just reached sixteen years of age, her eyes flashing with rage.

"Oh?" Zöpa looked at the girl with surprise and fear. Goodness! Can this be true or is it a dream? The hairs on Zöpa's body and the hairs on his head stood up simultaneously and because anger and fear arose together, even his calves were trembling.

"No, I've never had a gun."

Irritated, Lhündrub signed to Küntu Sangmo and led her quickly outside the assembly hall.

After a while, Lhündrub returned carrying a long gun. Goodness! It was an old-fashioned British rifle. It was covered with a thick layer of dust and on its butt there was still a mark left by five fingers. Probably that mark had been made by Lhündrub when he fetched the gun.

The people assembled there looked angrily at Zöpa and even though some of the older wiser ones were discussing and whispering to each other, not a single word could be heard.

"That's not mine. Really, that's not mine."

While Zöpa said this with tears in his eyes, two young men grabbed him by his shoulders and led him away.

"I don't own a gun. I've been done an injustice. I've been done an injustice... ..."

He was beaten three times causing him to become unable to move his leg which had swollen. His whole body was covered with black marks. "Who could hold such a grudge against me? What have I actually done wrong?"

By the time Zöpa was later proved innocent, his left leg had become crippled. It became a witness to one period of history.

Zöpa followed his daughter moving forward lamely, his leg aching. Looking at the small foot path in the middle of the forest enveloped by thick fog and at Küntu Sangmo's back, his eyes turned hazy and he felt hopeless about the future course of his life.

"In my opinion it would be better, if we both turned back. Even if we go to the hot springs, this leg of mine won't get any better. Now that the system of taking responsibility for production has been introduced, our field... ..."

"Don't think too much and be quiet. Tomorrow we will arrive at the hot springs of Dragkar."

Three

How fast time goes! A year passed in the blink of an eye. The natural beauty that signals the arrival of summer is now clearly visible on the grass plain of Dragkar. However, today the wide earth is not covered with a veil of fog. Lush green grass fills the earth in all directions and beautiful flowers are blooming in the passes and valleys. A young girl is carrying a wooden water barrel and is walking towards a foot-hill on the other side where there are five or six nomad tents. Oh, who is that girl wearing a nomad dress? During this time last year, I did not see a girl like her on the grass plain of Dragkar. I see! It is Küntu Sangmo!

Her face has a reddish glow and is youthful. Her eyes look joyful and both her body and mind give an impression of well-being. She takes slow steps and many thoughts are passing through her mind. Once in a while she bites her lips and sometimes she smiles openly. If you did not know her, you might well think that she was mad or at least had gone slightly crazy. However, she is a girl with all her five senses intact, possessing a sharp wit. Her loose character is well-known to everyone around. She is a woman who does not mind mixing with hundreds of men, no matter whether it is on the hills or in the plains.

In the previous year, Küntu Sangmo had brought her father to the hot springs of Dragkar and not long after she met Söbhe. She deceived her father with various lies and married Söbhe. As Söbhe was an illegitimate child, it was difficult to decide who his father was and there was also no need to decide it. Söbhe's mother was a dignified woman and after his birth, she kept her dignity and did not search for a husband. She put all her hopes in her only son and went on with her life. Generally, although mother and son lived a happy life and Söbhe was as honest and straight as an arrow, he took delight in gossiping and was not able to be self-sufficient. Moreover, he was not good-looking and, since a corner of his right nostril was missing, everybody, irrespective of whether they were young or old, called him Söbhe 'Yak with a Pierced Nose'.[121] Because of the defects of his physical faculties, he did not attract young women and had had to remain a bachelor until he reached the age of thirty years.

The previous year, Söbhe had gone to the hot springs and stayed there for a few days. By good fortune he had got to know Küntu Sangmo and, after only a couple of days, he had welcomed her to his home and made her his wife. At that time the joy in Söbhe's mind had been beyond any expression.

"Ah, Sangmo, you are like a heavenly goddess. You have cleared away all the agonies from my mind and from tomorrow on, I Söbhe, won't hesitate to run down the steepest paths to hell, if you ask me to, or to hit even my father's head if you ask me to."

"Söbhe, you're a really good person."

"You won't change your mind?"

"How could it change? Don't worry about that."

"Ah, this happiness of mine! Where can I fit my happiness?"

"Ha, ha!"

"It's true. It's true, yah!"... ...

A smile spread over Küntu Sangmo's face. Those past events made her feel more joyful and even though she was utterly moved by the sincere love Söbhe held for her, one thing that caused her unhappiness was her mother-in-law. Generally, it is very difficult for a bride and a mother-in-law to get along well. Küntu Sangmo's mother-in-law Lhatsho was a dignified old woman. Küntu Sangmo was jealous of her and that cruel old woman who had reached the age of sixty, still did not wish to hand over to her control over the household. Küntu Sangmo's jealousy of her mother-in-law turned into feelings of resentment and as the mother-in-law had an angry nature and was harsh in her speech, she also felt quite frightened.

"Ts...ts...! As I'm the mother of a son now, why should I fear you cruel mother-in-law."

Küntu Sangmo was carrying water and as she walked along, thoughts like these arose in her mind and she decided that by some means she should try to wrest control from her mother-in-law's hands by using a clever strategy.

"I must be a fool! Isn't it easy? As Söbhe is there, why should I worry? You cruel woman! The two of us will slowly eat the roasted barley flour, and we shall gradually see who is the winner!"

The beads in the rosary of days passed by one-by-one. The extent to which Küntu Sangmo abused and mistreated her mother-in-law grew worse and worse. In the beginning, when she offered tea to her mother-in-law, she only added a small piece of butter to her cup.[122] Gradually, the amount grew less and less and now she was only given tea without butter. First Lhatsho, the mother-in-law, became very displeased and she even reprimanded her daughter-in-law, who did not show any loyalty but scolded her back. The mother-in-law was slowly forced to become patient and not to oppose her daughter-in-law. Except for once, she did not tell her son about the way in which her daughter-in-law was limiting her food. Söbhe's mind would anyway have taken his wife's side. As the proverb says: "When an excellent horse gets old, it does not have any value. When one's parents get old, they won't be appreciated." She thought that now there was nothing to do but to experience her own miseries, but as she did not wish to bear this kind of torment from her daughter-in-law, she thought it would be better to live separately.

Her idea fitted in with Küntu Sangmo's wishes like a running horse. Although Söbhe first begged his mother to stay on, Küntu Sangmo said "If you need a mother, I'll take to the road with our small son." On hearing that Söbhe immediately agreed with her.

Lhatsho, the mother-in-law, who had passed her fifties and had reached sixty years of age had to move out. Actually, she was entitled to take possession of the family tent and all the property, and at least half of the household good belonged to her. However, kind parents have hearts as pure and soft as clean white wool. Despite being tender-hearted, she found her son Söbhe incapable and pathetic and her great concern for this son calmed her down, so she took only a torn old nomad tent left by her parents, who had lived in the old society, and a small number of essential things like a manual drill, a large ladle and a scoop. Söbhe had requested again and again that she would leave the only riding horse for Küntu Sangmo, and in the end she gave it to her unwillingly. Even though her livelihood was poor, because she did not have to bear the threats and abuses of her daughter-in-law, Lhatsho felt much happier. Due to her years,[123] her legs were not in such a good condition. However, she would still be able to take care of herself for another three or four years. If she couldn't, she would be able to borrow[124] from the villagers and people of the community. There was no need to worry about one's food, clothing and legs... ..... Thinking like this, Lhatsho considered that it was right for her to live separately. "You stray bitch, you will be paid back for your actions", and she cursed her daughter-in-law.

Four

The sun had just risen over the eastern horizon. On the meadow filled with blooming flowers of various colours, a young man on horseback was approaching Söbhe's household. The watch-dog Gyali, seeing a stranger arriving, barked and pulled on his chain and the iron chain was jingling. Küntu Sangmo's face was full of smiles and with her small son under her arm, she went to welcome the arrival. "Ghost dog! Be quiet!" she said threateningly to the old dog as she looked over her shoulder. The rider had arrived near the tent. Immediately when Lhatsho heard the barking of the dog, she looked cautiously out from the gap in her torn tent and cursed "Bitch, bitch!". Then without thinking anything more, she withdrew to squat on her leather carpet.

"Kelbhe, why haven't you come recently to see this mother and son? Have you forgotten us?"

"By no means. I accomplished the task and I didn't have any time to come."

"Go inside, go." After Kelbhe had entered the tent, Sangmo offered him a cupful of tea.

"Come! Come here, Daddy's dear child." Kelbhe took a piece of candy from his pocket and took the child from Küntu Sangmo's lap. This is what he said as he gave him the piece of candy.

"Speak in a low voice. They will hear out there." Küntu Sangmo said pointing her lips to the direction of Lhatsho's tent.

"Look, mouth and nose and everything are exactly like mine! Ha!"

"You are rejoicing too early. He says the child looks like him. He is truly an unlucky fool. When somebody else has left a child behind, he still calls it his own and rejoices over it. Let that old fool serve as a watch-dog," Küntu Sangmo said proudly and asked "Well, have you decided?"

Kelbhe shook his head. "It's really difficult. That ghost of an old woman said that she will never let me go unless I kill her. I don't have any way to do it. Eh... we two already have three kids... ..."

"Well, if you cannot break up with her, what is the good of grand words? Your words are as grand as a statue, but when you act it is nothing but snot. All right, take your child today and go!"

"I really don't have any other way. If it were not like that... ..."

"You don't have to explain. The moment you open your mouth, I can see what's in your mind."

The discussion ended. Kelbhe, leading his horse, went back the way he had come and, as before, the watch-dog barked loudly. Küntu Sangmo followed him with her eyes, looking angrily at his back. "Ts...ts...! That's all right. I shall look for a better person than you."

Küntu Sangmo was speaking to herself. Does Söbhe know that secret? Oh dear! Women are really possessed by a demon. Söbhe—that kind, humble and unfortunate husband, will have to live all his life deceived by this she-ghost.

The sun was about to hide behind a western mountain. The rays of the evening sun spread on the slate mountain of Dragkar and it rose shining towards the sky like a golden *stūpa*. On the grass plain the men were trying to gather their herds of cattle and sheep and from near by a herd of sheep was slowly approaching. Küntu Sangmo, recognising them as Söbhe's sheep, quickly lit the fire and boiled tea. From the outside, she appeared a truly affectionate wife devoted to her husband.

Küntu Sangmo swept clean the inside of the tent and cleaned Söbhe's cup with ash.[125] Then she wiped it with the end of her belt and poured tea into it for her husband to drink. When she had done that, she heard the watch-dog that was tied up outside the tent barking again. "Bad dog! You seem to be senile today. Don't you even recognise your master?"

Threatening the dog, Küntu Sangmo came out of the tent. About two hundred yards away[126] two people were approaching, one behind the other. Immediately on looking at them she recognised that the first one was her husband Söbhe. Ah, strange, who could the other one be? Looking at his way of walking, it seemed that one of his legs was crippled. I have not come across any lame man in the few hundred kilometres around this small area of Dragkar Dzakang, neither have I heard mention of one. He must be a pilgrim. You stupid old fool Söbhe! What need is there to bring home a pilgrim whom you have met in the midst of no-where? As Küntu Sangmo watched her husband Söbhe and the lame visitor came nearer and nearer.

"Oh, dear! Am I seeing right?" Küntu Sangmo wiped her eyes with her sleeve and looked carefully at the visitor. Her eyes had not been mistaken—the visitor was her father Zöpa.

Over a year ago Küntu Sangmo had not felt like working in the fields, and using the condition of her father's legs as an excuse, she had come to the hot springs of Dragkar. When she met Söbhe there, she did not take care of her father, but went secretly to her husband's place. First she had thought that her father would come to look for her. The months passed away one-by-one, but not even her father's shadow appeared. Recently she thought that her father must have gone home and she felt peaceful in her mind. She remained happily engrossed only in her own well-being. However, what to do now, that the old lame man had unexpectedly arrived before her? Oh, dear! What to do now? After several thoughts had crossed her mind, she finally found a solution. This was it. Except for this, there was no other solution.

"Sangmo! Ah, my daughter! Sang...mo...!"

Zöpa called out with tears welling up in his eyes and his throat choking.

"A-la! What's wrong with this old-man? You worthless corpse!"[127] said Küntu Sangmo with astonishment in a nomad dialect.

"What? Don't you really recognise him?" said Söbhe in surprise.

"A-la, Söbhe! Who is this?"

"This is..., ... this is..., ... Hey! Who are you?"

"Me? I am Sangmo's father. My name is Zöpa. Sangmo, don't you recognise your father?"

"A-la, such a worthless corpse! Ha-ha-ha-ha... ...! He-he-he-he... ...!"

The sound of Küntu Sangmo's laughing and the barking of the watch-dog Gyali blended into one and tore at Zöpa's earholes like a sharp spear smeared with poisonous liquid and the sound struck the middle of his heart. Like an anaesthetic syrup, it caused Zöpa to lose his mind and turned him somewhat senile.

Küntu Sangmo signalled with her eyes to Söbhe and entered the tent. Söbhe looked angrily at Zöpa and followed Küntu Sangmo.

O heavens! Did you see that? Ho, ho! How unlucky I am! O heavens! O heavens! ... ..."

"Wow, wow!... ..."

The grass plain of Dragkar was filled with Zöpa's lamentations and the dog's barking. Under the remaining light from the west, an old woman supporting a lame old man walked slowly towards a small ragged tent. There were tears in that old woman's eyes. Oh, that was Söbhe's mother, Küntu Sangmo's mother-in-law... ...no, not so, not so. She was Lhatsho, the dignified mother-in-law.

Five

During that day, an unbelievable, amazing and strange rumour spread among the nomads of the grass plain of Dragkar. Men and women, young and old were talking about it. The essence of that rumour consisted of two basic points: firstly, Küntu Sangmo's whereabouts were not known. Secondly, Lhatsho and Zöpa had got married. According to some people Küntu Sangmo had gone in the direction of Thrika, but others held this to be untrue. They said that she would not dare to go to some other place leaving her husband and child behind. Anyway it was clear that Küntu Sangmo was no longer on the grass plain of Dragkar.

"Where has she gone?"

Söbhe placed his small son in the front fold of his coat and as he led the herd of sheep to a grassy place, he spoke to himself. Judging by the way his dark coloured face had turned pale and by his bloodshot eyes, it seemed that he had not slept at all that night. "It's impossible.

Since Küntu Sangmo is normally kind and affectionate towards me, how could she have dared to leave me? As there is this small son born from her flesh and blood, it isn't possible that she has left us both." As he thought in this way his mind uncontrollably turned unclear. "Oh, dear! Küntu Sangmo and I have lived together for one year but, since we have no marriage certificate, who will accept that she is my wife?" He felt great regret. However, after a while his regrets vanished like bubbles in the surface of water and he was filled with a conviction that his wife would certainly come back. Although he expected her day after day, and missed her from the depths of his heart night after night, not even his wife's shadow appeared. The marriage of Lhatsho and Zöpa irritated him inconceivably and the crying of Küntu Sangmo's abandoned son made him feel even worse.

Until he had had a child of his own, he had not realised the fact that he was deeply indebted to his mother for her kindness. Now he had to be both a father and a mother to this child. Moreover, he still had to go to tend the flock of sheep, fetch water, and there was no end to those and the various other household tasks. Oh, dear! It was time to churn the milk. Now, whatever happened, it was best for him to do it with his own hands. He dragged the churn in front of the stove and after closing the lid well, he took hold of the churning stick. He churned vigorously and the milk splashed out of the hole in the lid of the churn, which made his face look as if it had been white-washed. A stream of milk flowed on to his shirt, and covered it all over with white drops of various sizes. Angrily he churned the milk, and churning the milk he got more angry. Everywhere inside and outside the churn had turned white and gradually the milk drops fell on to the ground and streamed in front of the stove. He would not have the good fortune to eat butter. Just then his anger flared and he kicked the churn. Immediately, the churn overturned and fell on the ground and after shaking and trembling for a while, it lay there peacefully. From the hole in its lid, milk poured out and ran in a stream across the floor... ...

The two old people, Lhatsho, who had passed her fifties and was now in her sixties, and Zöpa, had a few months ago fetched a marriage certificate. At first the secretary and the officials of the commune had been amazed and the two old people were also obliged to feel astonished at their own actions and behaviour. However, as they had been united by the power of their past actions, they became husband and wife and formed a household during their old age. Even though their bodies were lacking the energy of youth, they had a truly affectionate attitude towards each other. Because these two old persons, who had been abandoned by their son and daughter, had the sincere wish to share their joys and sorrows, the secretary, laughing, gave them a marriage certificate.

Though they both were old, their thoughts of enjoying the happiness of a new life had not aged. Zöpa, in spite of being lame, was very skilful with his hands. Especially, since he was skilled in sewing various kinds of clothes, the two old people were able to get enough income. Lhatsho was an experienced housekeeper and took especially good care of the female cattle and horses and their young. They did not have to worry about butter and cheese. The sound of continuous laughter came from their ragged tent. A smile spread across the wrinkled faces of the two old people.

"I had better go and ask my mother." With the child on his back, Söbhe entered the ragged tent where the old man and woman were living.

"Mother, because I'm your son... ...."

Actually, after having thought the matter over for some days, he had planned to confess his mistakes to his mother and to speak about a reconciliation between mother and son. Now, he was unable to speak even one word coherently.

"Söbhe. I don't hold any grudge against you. The mothers of this world have tender minds. The one to blame is that cursed woman. You are not to blame. If you can tolerate us two old people, then the two of us, mother and son... ...."

When Lhatsho saw her only son's pained expression the earlier anger and grudges instantly vanished and an immeasurable feeling of compassion arose. Remembering the torment and abuse her daughter-in-law had heaped on them both, a look of agony came over her wrinkled face and tears fell uncontrollably one-by-one from her old eyes.

"Mother, you two old people are not at all to blame. From today on I also have somebody to call "father" and somebody to love as "mother". Fa...ther..."

Zöpa's eyes had tears in them and he was nodding his head. Two small tears ran down his skinny cheeks. His eyes became hazy. Before those hazed eyes, the father, mother and son with their young grandson on their lap were picking flowers on the wide spacious grass plain and far away at a distance of more than two miles,[128] a girl was riding off on her black donkey which was heading in the opposite direction. They were silhouetted against a red-coloured haze which stretched along the horizon.

Goodness! That's my daughter.

"Sang...mo...!"

As soon as Zöpa called out like this in a clear voice, his eyes became clearer and when he looked carefully, his grandson Tshelo was eyeing him and laughing.

A Girl with Her Face Concealed by a Scarf

Tenpa Yargye

This is a story which actually happened on the grass plain of Nachen. It is also a story which probably won't happen again in the future.

One

It was the time when Akhu Sangye's family's herd of sheep had migrated from their summer pasture land to the autumn pasture known as the Valley of Violets. The old man had pitched his tent and through the opening, while he was lighting a fire, he could see his daughter Dekyi near the flock of sheep.

That grazing ground called "Valley of Violets" covered only one point seven square kilometres, but there was no other place in the grass plain of Nachen which had more abundant grass and better water. It was one kilometre away from the village. When the system of taking responsibility for production had been implemented and all the chiefs of the villages of the entire *shang*[129] had assembled, the head of Village Number Seven, Dorje, had obtained the smallest of all the grazing grounds. The chief of the village, Dorje, had been educated in the Agricultural University's branch unit on the grass plain. This year he had reached the age of forty and had taken great responsibility for the agricultural work. His skill in other tasks could not be underestimated either. After he had been elected as the chief of Village Number Seven, he had put into practice the things he had learnt from the specialist works he had previously read. He had decided to make a change in the seriously degenerating condition of the grass plain and, rounding up the work force of the entire village, he had used as fertiliser all the manure from the sheep and cattle enclosures. This had been spread on the grass plain, and at the beginning of winter by channelling water from springs and brooks in the valley by the slate mountains to the arid grass plain, he had created an irrigation network. He had gathered donations from the people and had surrounded the area with an iron fence and divided it among the people according to the rules. In a few years time, the grazing ground of Village Number Seven had a plentiful water supply during all four seasons and its grass was growing extremely well, so that one could not even make out the calves, goats and sheep amidst the grass. The village which had before been poor, became the village with the highest income in the area of the entire *shang*. Many people from other villages felt jealous of its success.

There were three daughters in Akhu Sangye's family. Even though the eldest of them, Dekyi, was twenty-five years old, she had never shown any interest in the opposite sex since she had left her mother's womb. Many young men from her village and other villages had sung love songs to her, but she had not even looked at them once.

Dekyi always wore a red scarf which covered her entire face. Except for her two attractive eyes, no-one had ever seen the rest of her face.

Every night, young men while turning over in their warm, soft leather garments, made various guesses about her "secret": "Could she be hare-lipped? No, because the sound of her speech was clear. Could it be, that she did not have a nose? No, that couldn't be the case as the place where the nose should be was raised. Then... ..." they had to remain in uncertainty and not even one person could reveal her "secret."

When I visited Village Number Seven in the grass plain of Nachen for the first time, many young men crowded round me and said: "Teacher Tenpa Yargye, you are a town-person and since you have a lot of knowledge, you will certainly know this. Why does Dekyi not show her face to other people? We have sung her songs about our love, but she does not pay any attention to us. What do you think could be the reason for that?"

I just shook my head, and was unable to find any answer to their question.

Tashi Tshering was a really obstinate person. Lifting his thumbs in a pleading gesture to me, he said:

"Please, please! Teacher, please find a way to make Dekyi show her face to other people. We want to see what her face actually looks like. What could be the reason why she does not pay any attention to us?"

I asked them, "Even Dekyi ignores you, aren't there still two girls in her family younger than her?"

"Here in our grass plain, it is against the custom for a younger sister to marry before the older one," he said.

"Then, are there not any other girls apart from Dekyi in the grass plain of Nachen?"

"Huu...," he sighed deeply and repeated again: "Teacher Tenpa Yargye, the young men of this *shang* are in a really terrible situation. This highway across the grass plain has brought us many facilities and caused our girls to leave."

"What, are the girls leaving?"

"Um..., a few of them have gone to the town. Some of them—the rough drivers on the highway... ...those who have gone to the middle-school are like wild animals that have been put into an enclosure. They do not feel attached to the grass plain but always rush off to town and say that they have to take entrance tests for civil and factory services. Anyway..."

After he had said all this with a desperate expression on his face, he lowered his head. When I saw that, I felt a hot sensation at the tip of my nose.

In order to solve their "problem", I invented the following method. When I had finished supper on my second day there, I summoned all the young men and women of the village who were in their twenties to the house of the village chief Dorje. A-ma-ma! There were sixteen young men, but no more than four young women. Jewels,[130] look upon me! If they were to be shared, there would be only one young woman for every four men. A-ma-ma! I felt astonished.

In the clear white light of a lamp, which was run on solar-energy, I turned on a cassette-recorder and asked each girl to sing a song. I emphasised that it was important to pronounce the words clearly. That evening the young men felt extremely happy, and when they were not whispering among themselves, they were looking at me, signalling with their eyes and showing all kinds of expressions. The young women looked timidly at the recorder in my hands for a while and then lowering their heads they began to whisper, pressing their shoulders against each other. Only Dekyi stayed alone in her place, her head wrapped in a red scarf, and even I was unable to see anything, except her eyes. Those eyes had no special distinguishing features that were different from others.

My effort had proved fruitless and the young men's hopes had been dashed.

That evening Ache Lhamo placed a huge bowl of boiled mutton in front of me and Chief Dorje. We were drinking alcohol together and exchanging views.

Chief Dorje said:

"Under my supervision the whole grass plain has been improved. Now what still needs to be done, is to improve the level of the scientific understanding among the nomad population. I hope that you who are from the publicity department will spread some scientific understanding and modern technology in this nomadic area."

Next day I again summoned all the young men and women of the village in order to take a picture of them in the sun. This was also so that the young men could see Dekyi's face. Before taking the picture, I explained to them, stressing my words, that the photo would appear as an illustration in magazines such as "Photography of the PRC",[131] "The

Tibet Pictorial"[132] and "The Beautiful Northern Plain",[133] and that I would also enter it in photography competitions. Therefore, the girls should remove their scarves and try to look decent. The other young men and women did as I wished but Dekyi, even if it had been a question of life and death, could not be persuaded to remove her scarf, and nothing else could be seen but those two eyes which attracted the minds of men.

When I had taken their picture and arrived at chief Dorje's house, he prepared a jarful of butter-tea using a special machine, and while pouring the tea into my tea bowl he said proudly: "Teacher Tenpa Yargye, could you give some lectures in our village about scientific knowledge? Wouldn't it be good if you could give them an introduction to what is called scientific and what superstition?"

I lowered my head and after thinking for a while, I put my tea bowl on the table and when I looked up, he was still standing in the same place, his two eyes shining with hope, waiting for my answer. I nodded my head twice causing him much delight. Like a small child who has received a long-awaited rare present, he said "What luck we have." He jumped up out of joy and hit the top of his head on a small nail in one of the roof beams causing a slight wound. I thought of cleaning the wound immediately but waving his hand he said, "Do not clean it. This will remind me in future of the day when the doors of science were opened for my village. Actually, it is only a small wound."

Using the lunch break on the second day, I called a meeting of the people inside the cattle enclosure. This is how I started my speech to them:

"What is 'science'? It is a branch of knowledge about the natural environment and also includes the whole sphere of human knowledge. It forms the essence of the methods which people have employed and developed according to their needs in the struggle for production and in the class-struggle. What is 'superstition'? It is the undeveloped world view characteristic of the primitive societies whose ability to produce is badly lagging behind. To improve the scientific understanding of modern farmers and nomads is important. It is also important to spread civilisation among them. Nowadays the material development of your village has reached a high level and the annual income of each person is over thirteen thousand five hundred *yuans*. All the families are living in houses which have more than one storey. You have many amenities such as cassette recorders, sewing machines and there are also some of you who go to tend the herds riding a motor-cycle. Most of the families make their yoghurt and butter-tea in special machines for those purposes.[134] So, you should improve your understanding of science and as for superstition...,"

Before I had finished my speech, the nomads, brushing dust from their clothes with their sleeves, had got up and left one after the other. When they went they were murmuring things such as "What? Superstition... science?" An old man, after he had gone two, three steps, turned round and said sarcastically: "Teacher Tenpa Yargye-la, although your grasp of these things is high, it is questionable whether our "snow-goddess" flowers[135] of the grass plain will prosper, if they are planted in the greenhouses of your towns. If the pigs of your towns were to be employed as substitutes of our nomad-dogs, that would hardly work either, ha-ha!" he was laughing loudly. The others joined in.

"You... ...you... ...you all... ...hee...," uncontrollably, a long sigh escaped from my lips.

At the end, there was nobody but me and Chief Dorje in the cattle enclosure.

Chief Dorje, as if he were suffering from an attack of epilepsy, was supporting his cheek with his hand, and remained quite still. Even his mouth and eyes were motionless.

When we got home, he fell on his bed in the way a balloon which had lost its filling of air collapses and he said,

"In your opinion, is there any other way?"

"They agreed to transform the grass plain under your leadership, but now, when they are told about science, far from accepting it, they are showing various signs of dislike. Really, ... " I was feeling utterly amazed.

"That is because they knew there would be benefits from transforming the grass plain," said Chief Dorje all of sudden, getting up.

"At first I showed them grass grown on dog shit. Because the dog shit had so much power, the grass grew very long and thick. On that occasion I explained to them the benefits of manure. That was something which they could see and apply, and they had no other option than to agree."

A-la-la! Nomads! Our nomads!
Praised for your industriousness and intelligence
You do not accept anything which is not obvious
Why do you accept the deities and spirits?
E-ma! This world!

The world under your dominance
Is actually like a piece of clean white paper.
Moving the pen of your intelligence on it
You write about deities and spirits
They are all under your control.
Do not forget to use ink!

The Tibetan people on these pages—are drawn from my diary of travelling to the grass plain of Nachen.

Feeling sad, I reluctantly returned to the town next day. This is not the end of the story.

Two

As soon as I got to my office, I took the time to begin writing a research report about Village Number Seven of the Nachen administrative area. I described how Village Number Seven had in an exemplary way transformed the seriously degenerated condition of the grass plain and also about what had happened due to their poor knowledge of science. After I had typewritten my report, I submitted it to the town-committee and to the local people's government, the board office for tending live-stock, the head-office of the Science Academy, the board office of people's religious affairs, the co-operative society and other related departments.

On Sunday some of my friends from Beijing visited me. They were all friends from the time when I had been studying in the university, and as we had not met for about nineteen years, I made elaborate preparations for their visit. As we had not met for so many years, there was a lot to discuss. They told me about recent developments in Beijing, about the Wangfujing market-place and the Xidan shopping-complex, and how beautiful the twenty-first century hotels and the Asian games village were. I recounted my experiences in Village Number Seven of the *shang* of Nachen and they listened like children taking delight in a story. Sometimes they frowned and sometimes, uncontrollably, they let out a long sigh as they shook their heads. After they had listened to that story which was both amusing and saddening, Jamyang Sherab, the editor-in-chief of "People's Pictorial",[136] who belonged to the first generation of Tibetan photographers, wanted to see the photos I had taken in Village Number Seven of Nachen and my wife handed him the photo-album. After taking a gulp of the wine I had offered for him, he stroked his hair as he carefully looked through the pages. Then, suddenly, as if he had found an incomparable treasure, he examined the photo of Dekyi and asked incredulously:

"Did you take this one too?"

"Yes, I took all of these pictures."

A big smile spread over Jamyang Sherab's face and the little wrinkles that spread from the corners of his eyes, like the fins of a fish, turned into two small fans with laughter. "This is great, great! It's really an outstanding achievement!" This is how he praised it, and they all gathered around the picture. "Wonderful! It has high artistic quality and an unusual theme," they said approvingly and devoured it with their eyes.

When they were about to leave, Jamyang Sherab took the photo and its negative and promised to publish it in his magazine. He also encouraged me, saying that if I really tried, I could make a career.

After half a year I received a copy of the "People's Pictorial" which they sent to me. On one of its pages Dekyi's picture was clearly printed and the title read "The two eyes of the girl from Jangthang." Moreover, there was also a short introduction to me stating that "Tenpa Yargye is a young writer skilled in literary composition and photography."

Even more unbelievable, at the end of the year Dekyi's photo won the gold medal in a photography competition called "Beauty of the High Plain". Of course, I took some interest in photography and had thoroughly researched this art. However, I got very confused about the fact that I had now accidentally won a gold medal and the question about the nature of photography caused me to become entangled in a net of doubts. Actually, I had taken that picture carelessly for the sake of the young men in Village Number Seven of Nachen *shang*, and had not paid any attention to its theme and artistic qualities. And I had not had any plans to enter a competition. However, it had become an achievement which I could always count on in times to come.

"It is true. Theory and practice must go hand in hand," said my wife who is skilled in giving advice.

Three

That day Dekyi was tending the herd of sheep in the meadow and was spinning wool. Tashi Tshering, Dawa Tashi and Tagnag had joined forces. The plan was that Dawa Tashi and Tagnag, pretending that they were collecting dung, would slowly approach Dekyi while talking to each other, and that Tashi Tshering would secretly come from behind and remove her scarf. Dawa Tashi and Tagnag, both carrying a sack, collected dung in not far away from Dekyi. Tashi Tshering, wearing white rubber-boots, was approaching Dekyi slowly, his back bent like a hunter stalking a wild animal.

At that moment Dawa Tashi and Tagnag, both carrying a sack full of dung, arrived in front of Dekyi and said, "Ache Dekyi, a good day for grazing! As you have spun so much wool, will you knit a sweater for each of us? Or... ...," and they put their sacks on the ground.

"Hee-hee!" said Dekyi pointing at Tagnag's sack of dung, "Why are you collecting shit? Hee-hee!" she laughed.

Tagnag turned round and looked, "My goodness! How dirty! One dry piece of shit has got into the dung-sack. While I was looking at Dekyi and Tashi Tshering, I picked up anything that came in my hands and so I collected this piece of human excrement. My goodness! How dirty!", he said.

"Hee-hee-hee!" Dekyi was laughing so violently that it even caused a pain in her stomach. "Hee-hee-hee... ... !" Pressing her stomach with both hands, she stood up and noticed the enemy approaching from behind.

Tashi Tshering, not knowing what was so ridiculous, felt deeply disappointed and was not even able to draw back his extended hand but remained stuck still as if drained of life. Dekyi said: "Yah! It's Tashi Tshering."

"Aa... ...aa... ... it's me," and with these words, Tashi Tshering was able to withdraw his hand.

"Hee-hee!" Dekyi laughed and went off towards the herd of sheep. The three young men were speechless and remained looking at Dekyi's thin and slender figure.

That evening Tashi Tshering, who was firmly resolved to reveal the secret of why Dekyi was not showing her face to others, put the white rubber-boots on his feet, and an inside-out sheepskin coat on his body. Having created a moustache from a yak's tail, he disguised himself as a terrifying ghost. Carrying a flash-light in his hand, he slowly crept towards the tent of Akhu Sangye's family.

Barking loudly, that dreadful black-dog was running towards him, like a wolf who has seen a sheep. He immediately threw a lump of meat at it, which he had prepared well in advance. The black-dog went away eating the meat, and he sighed with relief. Slowly he opened the door and as he was entering, he hit his foot against a wash basin which gave out the sound "ta-lang!"

"A thief has come! Catch that thief! Oh, dear! It's a ghost, a ghost. It's really a ghost. I saw its face covered with fur. ... ... I... ... I saw the thorns covering its entire body. Even our dog hasn't caught it. It must really be a ghost."

Saying so, all the members of Akhu Sangye's family were frightened and clung to each other.

Next morning Akhu Sangye noticed some clear footprints beside the door and said: "As a ghost does not have footprints, it was surely a thief," and thus the matter was decided.

Next day Akhu Sangye made a special dog's chain consisting of four springs, each about half a meter long,[137] and a similar number of rubber bands each of the length of about two feet[138] cut from the tube of a tyre. He joined the springs with rubber bands making them into a long chain which measured nine meters, and could be stretched upto twenty-seven meters, if a dog pulled hard. He stuck a dagger in the ground in the middle of his tent and making the dog sleep across the threshold, he firmly resolved to catch that "thief".

The chief of the village, Dorje, advised people to be on guard continuously, and for the next few days nothing happened.

Then one night Tashi Tshering again disguised himself as a terrifying "ghost" and broke into Akhu Sangye's tent a second time.

That evening there was dim moonlight covering the earth, and the high plateau between the mountains in four directions was silent like the silent waves of the ocean, and fearsome looking as there were dark clouds spread over the horizon. He crept along slowly remaining hidden and when he got near the nomad tent, not noticing anything apart from the barking of the dogs in the lower and upper parts of the village, he felt relaxed. Looking through his grandfather's magnifying spectacles which he was wearing, so that he could see Dekyi's face clearly, he slowly moved his left leg forward and holding a flash-light in his right hand, he opened the door of the tent cautiously with his left hand. Just then, with a loud bark, the black dog jumped on him.

"Thief! A thief has come. Catch him!" The three girls had just woken up and throwing on their sheepskin coats, they rushed to the door. About five or six steps away the black dog was holding down something greyish and biting at it. The three girls took hold of the dog's neck and pulled it up. "Oh, dear! Father!" the three girls exclaimed and ran back inside the tent in horror.

It seemed that before Akhu Sangye had fallen asleep, he had heard the sound of steps from near the door and the black dog jumping somewhere outside. Then, he got out from his sheepskin and while he ran towards the sound, Tashi Tshering had already escaped and was far away. The dog had not recognised its owner, and had jumped on him and bitten him. Since the wound it had caused was not big, it healed in a few days after musk had been applied to it.

How strange was the mirage which vanished like a flying bird and the dog that jumped on its owner. The body and face covered with thorns and fur, which had been seen previously, caused a rumour to spread everywhere in the village that it was not a thief but a ghost. Moreover, because footprints had been seen by the door, it was said to be a modern ghost.

For Akhu Sangye a ghost is an entity that exists when he thinks it does and doesn't exist when he denies it. In the past people destroyed monasteries and temples, burnt scriptures and condemned the role of lamas and monks, but there had been no ghosts. However, today people have an opportunity to live a secure and happy life under the admirable policies of the government, yet many people say that deities and ghosts exist and therefore that must really be the truth. Oh, dear! That modern ghost is not just an ordinary one. This black dog, possessed by a spirit, bit its owner. Goodness! The modern ghost also has footprints. When Akhu Sangye got that far in his thoughts, he began to shiver. And again he was lost in thoughts: "Holding guns in their hands the local guards

... Attention! Men of the People's Liberation Army, keep this in your minds! ... There are three unviolable rules and not one or two ... eight things to which you should pay attention and not six or seven."

When all the village had heard the news about the arrival of a modern ghost in Akhu Sangye's family, even the tantrics and oracle-mediums said, "We cannot tame a modern ghost."

Akhu Sangye, reciting *mani*-mantras, got furiously angry and not listening to his family, took a knife out of its sheath and killed the black dog that was "possessed by a spirit." After that, using his own skills, he made a wooden gun and a complete set of Chinese clothes out of leather. Then, one day, he placed the photo of Li Peng in front of himself and studied how to hold a gun.

From the second day, singing the song called "The three great rules and the eight points to pay attention to" he walked back and forth in front of the door to his home and at nights he stood by the door like a clay statue and protected his home. Since then, the modern ghost did not cause any harm to his family.

Four

"My goodness, it's so white!"

The crowd on the Barkor in Lhasa had surrounded a girl and were staring at her. It was exactly as though they had seen a strange thing, not heard of before in this world.

That girl's face was whiter than a wall that has just been white-washed and softer than the face of a new-born child. Even the pores of her skin could be discerned so clearly, that nobody since their birth had ever seen such a face before. Some people, not believing their own eyes, stretched out their hand and lightly touched the girl's face. Some people suspecting that she had a skin disease or a disease caused by blood deficiency did not dare to go near her. The exceedingly long hairs on top of the girl's upper lip were exactly like the moustache of a lucky trader.

The girl was standing like a fool in the midst of the crowd giggling in embarrassment.

The girl whose white face was adorned by a moustache for a while became the main topic for the people of Lhasa, who take delight in discussing rumours in tea-houses.

Some of them said that she was a certain film-actress playing the main character of a particular girl in a particular film. She was also the director of that film X and is called... ...... They acted as if they were thinking about it.

Also some of them said that "She is a famous actress of the Autonomous Region who acts in television. That moustache is an artificial one. She is called Dekyi. She and I ... ."

And some said... ...

Finally, some people even claimed that she was a human being from an other world.

I have to beg your pardon. Except for her name, you have not come to know who she actually was—that girl was Dekyi, the eldest daughter of Akhu Sangye's family from the grass plain of Nachen.

The winter time is the most relaxed time for the nomads. They call it "the season of pilgrimage". During that season, they flock towards the south like birds.

When Dekyi first arrived to Lhasa, the weather had been so hot, that she had had difficulty breathing and both her eyes had turned misty due to the stream of perspiration running down. Still, she had wrapped her head in the scarf and continued like that for three days.

No one else in the town had wrapped their head like her. Everyone looked very active.

After three days, since she was having difficulty breathing, she had been forced to remove that red scarf.

In April 1992, when I, the author, visited the grass plain of Nachen for the second time, Akhu Sangye was as before holding that wooden gun in his hands and standing with a brave expression in front of the village.

I asked him "How long will you be standing like this?" To which he replied "I will stay like this until the year 2000."

This is a story which happened some time ago in the grass plain of Nachen. Could it happen again in the future?

The Yellow Leaves of Summer

Tashi Palden

One

Some parents in the countryside have such a deep love for children they choose to have many sons and daughters. Even though they know that later on their upbringing will cause great hardships. They have a natural aversion to sending their children to go as baby-sitters for others. They think that though people these days use the pleasant-sounding title "baby-sitter", it's actually no different from being a servant. In their opinion children will be happier staying close to their parents, eating and drinking with them, even if they share nothing more than *tsampa* balls[139] and black tea and their food and clothing are poor.

However, some people don't think like that; they hold that a girl's life will turn out happier if she is sent to a town, irrespective of what work she does, and that she will be admired and able to take pride in herself. Moreover, many young girls consider such an opportunity something marvellous, a dream beyond their reach, pondering on how nice it would be if they had a relative or acquaintance who would one day invite them to work in a town.

Before she became a baby-sitter for her elder sister Pasang Yangki, Nyidröl went to the central primary school of the *shang*[140] and she also harboured hopes of that kind. She thought about the delights of urban life, which she had heard from her schoolmates and teachers, about the multi-storey buildings which were so high that if you gazed right to their top your hat would fall off your head. The highways with their mirror-like and even surfaces. The wondrous goods for sale, beautiful as flowers. The crowds of people, as attractive as gods and goddesses, milling like ants scattered from their nest. The eternally shining lights and amusements at night, and especially the many delicious things to eat like rice dishes, *momos,* sweets, apples and other delicacies available, throughout the four seasons. All these images arose hazily in her imagination and captivated her mind. Some girls who had been her classmates had left the school and gone to towns and cities, she dearly wished to do so too and her mind was completely absorbed by the thought. Her hopes were not just empty dreams as there was a basis for real optimism. She had an elder sister who, after finishing her schooling, had got work in a town, and so she thought that she would also one day get the chance to go there.

In the second year after her sister married her family received a letter from her sister in which she did indeed write about Nyidröl. The letter said that she and her husband were busy with their work and because neither had their parents near them Nyidröl should be sent there to look after their two children and they would take care of her future prospects. Nyidröl was thrilled and proudly told her schoolmates that she would soon be going to a town. Moreover, her mother agreed that she could go and thought she should leave almost the very next day. Her father didn't feel so certain about it and said, "If it does not turn out well, the younger daughter will bear the losses." He was worried about Nyidröl's future.

The mother imagined her elder daughter so busy with her government job and work at home that even if her hair caught fire she would not have time to put out the flames. Especially she visualised her grandchild crying amidst shit and piss to get attention. She pooh-poohed her husband's doubts saying, "Even if we send Nyidröl to school, it isn't the same these days. We will have to find a way in by the backdoor, which for the child of a farmer like us is as difficult as trying through the proper channels. In any case she will become a peasant. Instead of that, if we send her to her sister it will not only benefit her for the time being but also in the long run. It will also make life less difficult for Pasang Yangki." As for Nyidröl, this was the realisation of her dreams. Even if she were to seek it out this kind of opportunity wouldn't come her way again. Wanting to leave immediately, Nyidröl became very excited and restless, and since she was worried that her father wouldn't let her go, she lied to him and said, "It's really so. However much I study, I won't learn anyway. Probably I was a donkey in my previous birth."

TWO

When she received the letter Nyidröl was a small girl, about ten years old. Some years later, her sister's two children had become big. The older one was going to primary school and the other was about four or five. Also, Nyidröl had turned into a budding adolescent. Nowadays her sister and her brother-in-law both called her "Aunty" imitating the way the two children usually referred to her. That conveyed a sense of intimacy and belonging, and therefore Nyidröl was very pleased at being addressed in this way.

The two children had now grown up to the point where there was no real need for a baby-sitter. The fact that Nyidröl's body and her mind were undergoing changes made both Tredön and his wife think that it was now time to decide on her future. There had even been some men who had asked to marry her, but all of them had only mentioned the topic incidentally, along with other matters, and none of them had actually come with *chang*[141] to make a marriage proposal. As it was impossible to guess whether they wanted to propose to her seriously, or had only been joking about it, there was nothing else to do than wait for them to come again with 'the *chang* for requesting the bride's hand' since Tredön and Pasang didn't dare to take the initiative and ask such suitors whether they actually wanted to marry Nyidröl.

Tredön knew a bachelor called Sithar, who was working in a road construction office. For some time he had been saying teasingly to Nyidröl "This is my bride." Moreover, he had also spoken in a joking tone to Pasang Yangki requesting her to give him Nyidröl as his bride. Sithar was heavily built and his eyes were small, his nose big and his skin black and pockmarked. Nyidröl used to call him "Uncle", and when she was small she had even been frightened of him. Though he was thirty-six or thirty-seven, he was still a bachelor. It caused him immeasurable mental anguish that none of the girls in the neighbourhood showed any interest in him. Though he felt deeply depressed that his parents had not provided him with better looks, there was no way to correct that and he had no other allure than to become rich to see whether he could attract people by his wealth and by giving up tobacco and alcohol. Nowadays the people in his office were trying to guess how much money he had. He had built his own house, on an area covering three hundred square meters. He lived in his office and had let the house out for rent. Since Pasang Yangki and Tredön thought that there was a big age difference between them and their appearances were as different as earth and sky, they took his overtures as something of a joke and ignored them.

Nyidröl grew up in the course of time and Tredön took responsibility for her welfare just as he did for his two children. Before, Pasang Yangki had washed his underwear and socks, but nowadays he saw Nyidröl searching for them of her own accord and washing them. When Pasang Yangki heard about the many cases of baby-sitters ousting their mistresses, she became alert to the invisible danger lying in Nyidröl's body and got slightly worried about her. Around that time Sithar arrived at just the right moment carrying tea, *chang* and presents, and actually asked for Nyidröl as his bride. Pasang Yangki hesitated and said, "I will ask the person concerned."

Pasang Yangki said to Nyidröl, "There is a saying 'If you wish to be happy later in your life, look for an old man as your husband.' If you agree to marry him, you won't have to worry about food and clothing during your entire life and you will have a house of your own. Luxuries of that kind are difficult to find even if you search for them with a golden lamp."

Nyidröl interjected, "Please don't tell me that I have to rush to become that ugly-looking man's bride. It's better to become a nun than to get married to a man like that."

Tredön said, "You can't really blame Aunty. It's a crying shame if she is sent to be Sithar's bride. It would be so sad if Nyidröl, who's as beautiful as a peacock, is tied to a husband with pockmarks on his face."

Pasang Yangki retorted, "Do you imagine that you're so incredibly beautiful?", and she continued to Nyidröl, "When I was young I also thought a person's appearance was very important, but once you're married, and the children have been born, who has time to pay attention to someone else's face? Whether her husband is as handsome as Gesar[142] or as ugly as a pig. All that matters to a woman is if he is sincere and affectionate towards her and takes responsibility for supporting her."

Tredön teased her and laughed, "Then, are you saying that I'm a pig?" To which Pasang Yangki sarcastically shot back, "Oh, my dear! Aren't you King Gesar?"

Sithar was thinking that even though Nyidröl was beautiful, as she was a baby-sitter and didn't have any chance of getting work in an office, she would probably not refuse. Moreover, when he met Nyidröl he said jokingly, at the same time watching her expression, "My girl, if you become my wife, even though I can't make you a noble lady you won't have to feel inferior to other girls. Do you want to come?" Since Sithar had now actually come to ask for her in marriage, Nyidröl felt immediate repulsion for him and what sprang to her mind was, "Even my father is more youthful than you. Eat shit!" However, she didn't dare to verbalise the word "No". So, pretending that she was joking as usual, she said to him: "Old man, don't tease a child!" Her words struck home, and though he understood their message he didn't lose hope and approached them again, promising in front of Pasang Yangki that Nyidröl wouldn't have to go out to work and would live her whole life in happiness.

But Nyidröl had made her final decision not to get married to him. Therefore the couple could not do anything about it and Tredön tried to turn the matter around by diplomatically saying, "Sithar, don't be in a hurry. Nyidröl is still young and also, because our younger child can't manage by herself yet, we plan to keep her for one or two more years. Therefore, how about discussing this matter later?" Although Sithar wasn't pleased, he kept up a brave smile, saying, "Let me wait another year or two. But you shouldn't keep two." In the guise of a joke he was hinting at something.

Three

On hearing Sithar's words, Tredön felt a hot surge inside himself and his face became uncomfortable, as if it had been burnt by the sun. "To keep two?" When he thought about it he felt slightly more easy in his mind as he had never harboured such an idea until now. Of that he was completely certain, and he could even swear to it. However, he actually started to wonder how it would be if the two sisters could somehow be exchanged. Once this thought had arisen it soon gained force, like an electric current, and overwhelmed his consciousness. Every time he dwelt upon the completely different character, speech and behaviour of the younger and older sister, the idea became even more compelling.

When he had first got to know Pasang Yangki, before their marriage, she had also had a nice nature and all the people in the office had spoken about her enthusiasm for her work. After they married all her energies had turned to housework. When she became pregnant with her first child, Tredön had taken even greater care of her and paid much attention to her. He had done all the housework when Pasang Yangki chose to feign being tired. Moreover, after the birth of the child he would say, "It's not easy to give milk to the child", and take great care about her food and ensure that she could get enough rest.

During her maternity leave of four months, Pasang Yangki had learnt how to play mahjong, and even though she didn't play for big stakes she had got a taste for it and became fascinated by the game. She took part in all kinds of respectable and rowdy gatherings of her colleagues. Wherever Pasang Yangki went Tredön used to go to fetch her, and if he didn't arrive at exactly the right time she would look daggers at him and assault his ears with endless insults. Ever since Nyidröl had come to stay as baby-sitter she had got together with some friends to drink *chang* and play mahjong two or three times a week. They took turns at hosting these gatherings in their homes and gambled. However much Tredön advised her when she was about to give birth to her second child it was of no use, and she continued to go out gambling as before. The labour pains started early in front of a mahjong table and the baby was born before they reached the hospital. Afterwards she was holding the baby in her left arm and giving it milk, while her right hand was playing mahjong as she explained with pride to her new gambling friends the wonderful events that had taken place during the birth.

Even though Tashi Döndrub[143] felt angry and displeased about his wife's behaviour, whenever he mentioned it Pasang Yangki immediately said, "O.k. O.k. I know. From now on I won't touch mahjong again." She kept promising, but when it was actually time to go she gave some reasons why it would be wrong not to attend and made false promises saying, "Today I won't touch mahjong; I'll come home early." When she said this, he knew that her words were untrue, but he could do nothing about it. At last, Pasang Yangki's way of speaking and her behaviour became completely beyond his control. As he could do nothing to influence it, he had no other choice than to ignore it.

One day he had something important to do, but when it was time to leave Pasang Yangki had gone to an inauguration ceremony and Nyidröl was also out at the market. Neither of them had returned yet. So he got very agitated, not finding anybody to whom he could entrust his small child. When he looked at his watch, and saw that it was time to go, he could find no other solution than to lock his small daughter inside the house. All afternoon he felt uneasy, and as soon as he had finished work he rushed home immediately. Even though Nyidröl had returned after he left, when he heard that the little girl had knocked down and broken a thermos, he picked up his child and looked to see whether she was injured. Fortunately the thermos had fallen from the table on to the floor and not on the child, so she hadn't been hurt. "What the hell were you doing until so late?", shouted Tredön, enraged.

Nyidröl flashed back at him, "Well, where has my elder sister gone?" Tredön was angry and said, "There's nobody worthwhile in your family.

You are all leather straps cut from same skin. If you don't want to work, you can go back to your parents."

Although Nyidröl had felt frightened of Tredön when she was still a child, as she grew up she understood enough to be concerned about him, when she saw her sister's way of acting and his sheepish attitude. She had tried to take care of him in every respect and made efforts to compensate for her sister's negligence. Normally she was silent, diligent in doing the housework and very affectionate to their two children. The children called her "Aunty" and they were almost more attached to her than to their own mother. Today, when Tredön spoke to her like that, she was unable to bear it and burst out, "I went to the market to buy vegetables, and wasn't wandering around idly. When you can't control your own wife, there's no point in getting angry with the father and slapping the son. If you tell me to go, I shall go." Crying, she sorted out her clothes and packed them into a bundle.

Although for a while Tredön ignored what was happening, the small girl jumped down from his lap and clasping Nyidröl's legs pleaded, "Aunty, Aunty, don't go! Aunty, don't go!" Nyidröl explained to her, "Now, since both of you are grown up, there is no need of Aunty."

Tredön knew that his words had been too harsh, and actually he understood clearly that Nyidröl was not the one to be blamed for what had happened that day. So he admitted his mistake and apologised to her. Normally, except for complaining to her elder sister, she didn't mention anything to Tredön, but today she had scolded him and pointed out that he couldn't control his own wife. He felt almost as if his own younger sister had shown concern for him and was delighted and moved. Of course he'd noticed that she usually sympathised with him, and even though he had said today that the two sisters were leather straps cut from the same hide there was actually a great difference in their character, speech, behaviour, mental attitude and so on. As Nyidröl blossomed to adolescence her body bloomed fully with every protuberance and curve in the perfect place. Looking at this, and at her shining eyes, he admired her appearance and wondered how the two sisters could be straps cut from the same piece of leather.

Although they could have sent Nyidröl away with whoever came to ask for her hand, they both considered it an important and heavy responsibility to take care of her future. Tredön showed even more

concern and interest in Nyidröl's future than Pasang Yangki. He thought
that they should seriously look for a partner who really suited her like
"a tooth that fits in her mouth", and not just half-heartedly give her
away to anyone. If they did that they would regret it and it would be a
pity for her.

Four

It was raining outside. It was the first rain after some oppressively hot
days and the first heavy downpour of that year's rainy season. As time
passed, the sound of the water from the gutters dripping on the forecourt
got louder and louder and was irritating to Nyidröl's ears.

Normally, at times like this, Nyima Dölma's lively imagination
would drift back to her native place and she would visualise many
marvellous and beautiful things. In the morning, after a heavy rainfall,
thick fog would gather at the base of the mountain as if it was someone
who had yet to awake from sleep and all the earth was shining as though
it had been polished with oil. Fresh green shoots, as small as a lark,
with their heads bowed were well nourished by the nectar of rainwater,
like someone soundly asleep. Only after the morning sun and the cool
wind had wiped away the remaining drops of nectar from their surface
did the green shoots arise from their sleep and look alert. The sweet
sound of a lark's song made them rise, one after the other. The sound
reverberated everywhere and intoxicated the ears. The beauty and
enchantment of the fields immediately after rain were beyond
imagination.

However, this evening the sounds of thunder and rain seemed to
purposely irritate and injure Nyidröl. The small girl had caught a cold,
and for a few days the fever had interfered with her sleep and she had
been crying at night. This evening, as soon as she had got a little sleep,
Nyidröl had been disturbed by the sound of thunder and rain and had
to get up again and again.

As soon as Nyima Dölma had fallen into a pleasant slumber the
small girl started crying again. The sobbing penetrated the depths of
her sleep, and she knew that she should rise and struggled to shake off
her torpor. The bedroom of the parents was the interior room, beyond
the children's bedroom. Tashi Döndrub, who was sleeping there, was

awakened by the sound of the child's crying. Thinking that Nyidröl would get up, he waited for a while, but as nobody moved and the child continued crying, he couldn't stand it and got up. The rain was still falling, which had made the temperature in the house drop and an icy wind was blowing inside from a window that had been left open. He was not wearing anything besides his underpants and without even putting on his slippers he went barefoot to the child. First he placed his hand quickly on the child's forehead and then took her in his lap. He lulled the child for a while in his arms, checking whether she wanted to drink some boiled cold water. Slowly the child closed her eyes.

Although Nyima Dölma was deep in sleep some fear had entered her mind and in her dream she got up, picked up the child, and walked around. When she actually awoke she realised that this action had been only a dream and she felt that a long time had passed since she heard the child crying. She leapt up, alarmed, and opened the door to the children's bedroom. When she entered she met Tashi Döndrub who was just leaving. Nyidröl was wearing loose pyjama bottoms, and only a flimsy sleeveless undershirt. Immediately she saw Tashi Döndrub both her hands flew to her chest. At first Tashi Döndrub felt somewhat embarrassed; her breasts were white and erect, showing clearly between her flexible soft fingers. Her firm, well-shaped thighs could be seen through her diaphanous pants. He remained there, frozen, unable to move away. Even though Nyima Dölma felt ashamed, she was unable to leave at once and, after glancing quickly at him, she lowered her head. Immediately after that, even though their minds flashed around, like lightning in the sky, an invisible wall separated them and neither of them dared to vault it.

"I thought that Aunty was sleeping."

"I didn't know that you'd got up."

The small girl cried again and both of them were relieved of their embarrassment; without saying anything they moved towards the crying child.

"You go to sleep. I'll take care of her."

"Aunty, you haven't had much sleep yourself so you should go back to bed. I'll take care of her."

Both of them were trying to stop the other and reaching out towards the child. As Nyima Dölma was the more dexterous she was the first to lift up the girl. Drawing her close, she comforted her in her arms. Tredön stood beside her and together they attended to the child. "If you were not here how would I manage?" he said, moved. To which Nyima Dölma sarcastically replied; "What is the difference for you whether I am here or not? If I were not here, most probably you'd have got someone even better than me."

Wrapping a blanket around himself, Tredön sat down and, after lighting a cigarette, he said, "Where could one find someone better than you? I'm not belittling your sister, but sometimes I doubt whether you and Pasang Yangki really are sisters from the same parents."

Nyima Dölma said, "That is the result of your own bad habits. Actually, if I had work and could get a regular salary there probably wouldn't be this Nyima Dölma looking after children."

"Like the saying goes: 'An adult grows up from a child and a horse from a foal.' Even if you had work and earned a salary you'd be very different from your older sister."

After Nyidröl had taken the small girl in her lap, and lulled her in her arms for some time, she fell asleep. She slowly put her back into her bed and after she had finished with that Tashi Döndrub went to the toilet to have a piss and Nyidröl went back to sleep in her own bed. Across from the children's bedroom there was a corridor leading to the kitchen, toilet and the living room. When Tashi Döndrub went to the toilet his mind was like a river plunging into a deep abyss. When he came out Nyidröl was lying in her bed with her eyes open like the morning stars, looking at him silently.

For some time Tredön had had one thought in his mind which had caused him many nights of sleeplessness, but he had neither dared to express it, nor do anything about it. His thoughts were as agitated as flashes of lightning, his face was burning hot and it even seemed that he had difficulty in breathing. Suddenly he said, "I'm feeling very cold, let me in your bed." When these words had escaped from his mouth, he felt surprised at his own courage. But also he felt uncertain of what he should do if Nyidröl defended herself like a ferocious tiger. It was still raining outside, and with a cold brisk wind a few raindrops blew in through the window and fell directly on Nyidröl's face.

"If you're feeling cold you should take good care of the person who gives you warmth." Except for this rebuke, Nyidröl didn't defend herself nor did she show any signs of repulsion. He thought that she would get wet, and, feeling encouraged by that, started to get into her bed. Nyidröl grasped hold of her quilt and, except for saying "Don't you have any shame? I will shout!", didn't offer any real resistance. Tredön understood her inner feelings and without saying anything he jumped upon her like a wild tiger, pulling the covering away by force. Nyidröl lifted her hand as if she'd heard something, and said, "Be quiet. My sister is coming." Tredön was startled; his whole body turned cold and, holding his breath he listened attentively, but could hear nothing. Laughing, Nyidröl covered her head, and Tredön again pulled away the quilt and fell on top of her. Like the union of sky and earth, everything turned completely dark and in the midst of the fierce wind nothing except the sound of their heavy panting could be heard.

After they had performed their act of mad ecstasy everything became silent.

Five

It was still raining and the sound of it could be heard very clearly. Nyidröl was crying and Tredön felt alarmed. He asked, "What happened? Do you feel regret?" For a while Nyidröl didn't say anything; she only cried. It made him feel very worried and in fright he asked, "Do you regret it?"

"I'm afraid. If my sister comes to know about this, what shall we do?" said Nyidröl, turning her back to him.

Tredön said, "I see. That's what you're worried about. That mainly depends on both of us. Nobody except the two of us knows about this. If we don't let people notice, nobody will know about it."

"Aren't you afraid they'll come to know?" Nyidröl asked.

"I'm not afraid."

Nyidröl touched his face with her finger saying, "When my sister is stripping off your skin with her fingernails, let's see."

"I don't care if my skin is stripped. Not even if my heart is pulled out", Tredön responded. Embracing Nyidröl, he continued; "I know how much concern and care you've given me until now. I haven't been able to repay your kindness at all. However, I'm keeping all that firmly in my mind." Nyidröl said, "Indeed, in doing what I did for you I didn't have any other aim than to serve my master. Is this how you repay my kindness? Up till now no man ever touched me, but tonight I lost my virginity. If I've got pregnant, what shall I do?" Tredön answered, "Don't be angry. I don't in any way think of you as a servant. I admire you from the depths of my heart." Usually they were quite familiar with each other, and sometimes joked and teased each other in front of Pasang Yangki. Until now they had been separated by an invisible wall not trying to cross it, they had not even spoken about it. Now, suddenly, it was as if the wall preventing physical contact had been destroyed, and so the wall preventing them from speaking had evaporated by itself. They said anything that came into their minds. They had sex again, and afterwards Nyidröl told him, "Now, if you don't go to your own bed my sister might come." But Tredön said, "Your sister is probably still enjoying piling bricks on top of each other." He still didn't want to leave her. Nyidröl looked at the watch and it was almost three in the morning. The rain had stopped. She got worried, saying, "When my sister comes, will you dare to lie here?" Tredön got up unwillingly and, after giving her a kiss, went to sleep in his own bed.

After about fifteen minutes, Nyidröl heard someone with heavy-sounding steps climbing the stone stairs and knocking at the door. Tredön, being completely exhausted, had fallen asleep, but Nyidröl's mind was restless and, far from sleeping, she thought and thought and the more new thoughts appeared the more and more confused she became. Stretching out the wings of her imagination, she circled around the landscape of her own future. As soon as she heard the sound of knocking at the door she was slightly startled and felt as if a policeman was coming to arrest a thief. Her heart was beating fast and she didn't dare to get up immediately. But when she thought about it she realised that her sister did not know anything about the events that had just taken place. As she got up, scolding started from outside. A voice called, "Nyidröl! Nyidröl! You must be in a deep sleep." Nyidröl replied, "I'm coming," and as she opened the door even though her heart was still beating fast she rubbed her eyes, acting as though she was still half asleep. After Pasang Yangki had stepped in, she chided Nyidröl, "How can you be sleeping so heavily?" As Nyidröl was standing there in nothing but her underpants and undershirt, she said, "Goodness! Young girl, aren't you ashamed of wearing nothing but underpants?" Those words affected Nyidröl as if a handful of hot ashes had been thrown in her face, causing her to blush. She felt as cold inside as though a bucket of icy water had been poured into her, her heart started to beat faster. She almost stopped breathing. Pasang Yangki halted her scolding, opened the door of the other room, and remembering her children, asked, "How is the girl?" But, not listening to the answer, she went into the room. She took a glance at her children and kissed the hand of the younger one. After that she went directly to her bedroom, put on the light and closed the door. Nyidröl relaxed and, because she didn't dare to sleep, listened furtively to their talk.

Tredön had also woken up and, realising that Pasang Yangki had arrived, he used his hand to shield his eyes from the light of the lamp. He reproached her, "You're so late!" Pasang Yangki was half drunk and a strong smell of *chang* emerged from her mouth. Ignoring her husband's complaint she giggled, and lying back with her head on the pillow she said, "There was such heavy rain and I thought that you would come to fetch me. However, it seems that now people are flinging their arms round the neck of a beautiful goddess in the realm of dreams." Tredön wondered if Pasang Yangki had an inkling of anything. Although he felt frightened, he pretended to be angry, "I know you don't like me coming to fetch you. So how would I dare to?" Pasang Yangki answered, "Now, forget about that. It was good that you didn't come to collect me tonight. I'm in luck these days. Make a guess! How much did I win tonight?" But, Tredön had no interest in these matters and told her, "Go to sleep. It's very late."

When Nyidröl heard those words she imagined that her sister had certainly won a few thousand and she felt contempt.

Pasang Yangki said, "You want so much to sleep, but just for the fun of it I won't let you. I need it tonight." When Pasang Yangki was slightly drunk on *chang* she always said she needed it. Tredön got frightened and tried to avoid the demand by saying, "Now go to sleep. It's already so late. I have to get up early tomorrow." As Pasang Yangki was saying that she needed it, and Tredön was doing everything possible to avoid it, Nyidröl got worried and thought, "Why doesn't he get it over and done with by simply doing it somehow? He's such a stupid man."

Pasang Yangki playfully took hold of Tredön's "it", and because it was as lifeless as an old donkey enjoying the sun she grew angry and got up. "You probably have another one", she said, and went to sleep in the children's room. However much Tredön tried to get round her she ignored him and they fought for a while.

Nyidröl got even more frightened and thought, "Oh dear! He's such a stupid person!"

Six

The invisible wall, between Nyidröl and Tredön, had crumbled and they seized every occasion to be together, especially as Pasang Yangki continued to play mahjong whenever she had time. After they finished the housework, without any concern for the time of day, they created even more opportunities and they reached the stage where they did not want to separate from each other. Their actions were sliding towards danger and both of them were aware that one day Pasang Yangki would come to know about it. Even though they realised that there was a deep abyss in front of them, and that when they fell into it it was not certain whether they would be dead or alive, they didn't want to turn away from it and continued moving forward. Although they were lovers when they were alone, in front of Pasang Yangki and the children they were the master and the baby-sitter as before. So, for a while, Pasang Yangki didn't notice anything.

Most of Nyidröl's clothes were Pasang Yangki's old ones. Although a few new clothes were bought for her for celebrations and the Tibetan New Year, Pasang Yangki bought them and Tredön had paid almost no attention to this. However, now when he went to the market with Pasang Yangki to buy new clothes, he said to her, "Won't you buy something for Nyidröl too?" Once he went on an official trip to Chengdu, and when he got back he had bought long flannel shirts for both Payang and Nyidröl. He gave one to each of them, separately. As Payang didn't like the colour of her shirt, she said in front of Nyidröl, "My goodness! Aunty's shirt is a better colour than mine," and she held it up in admiration, wanting to exchange it. Normally Nyidröl would certainly have said right away, "It makes no difference to me. Sister, you choose." But now the fact that Tredön had done something thoughtful for her made her feel equal to her sister and, not wishing to trade shirts, she said, "I think that your shirt is good too." Payang felt disappointed and as soon as Nyidröl had gone to fetch the child from school she said sarcastically to Tredön, "You are behaving differently now. Have you got fed up with me?" Tredön said, "Since you are sisters, what does it matter who gets what? Aunty has worked for us for many years. Don't you feel any compassion for her?"

After the older child had finished his homework, Nyidröl put both the children to bed and Tredön stayed up watching television. Nyidröl arranged the children's clothes by their pillows so that they would be easy to put on the next day. After she had finished she still had to do the washing-up and she went into the kitchen and got started. In the television programme a small family had finished eating supper and the man was reading a book. The child was watching cartoons and the woman, washing the dishes, was speaking to the man. Watching the programme, a thought suddenly occurred to Tredön, "How good it would be if Nyidröl were the mother of these two children." Feeling moved, he called "Nyidröl! Nyidröl!" Nyidröl didn't hear him because of the sound of running water in the kitchen and because the door was closed. So he went into the kitchen and put his arms round her waist saying, "There's no hurry to wash the dishes. Rest for a while." Drawing her to him, he kissed her. Nyidröl had a bowl in one hand and, even though she pushed him away with her other hand, he was totally intoxicated with desire and was undoing the buttons on her shirt. Nyidröl got terrified and pushed him away with force, saying, "The children aren't even asleep yet. Aren't you ashamed?" As it was a strong shove, he fell and hit his waist on the counter for cutting vegetables. He shouted out in pain and pretended he couldn't get up. She got alarmed and, putting the bowl aside, tried to lift him to his feet. He then jumped on her like a ferocious tiger, embracing her and Nyidröl hugged him passionately in return. The water flowing from the tap drowned all other sounds and nothing could be heard. Nyidröl said, "I think it's best we stop this affair of ours now. If we don't it will get more dangerous." Tredön didn't like what he had heard and answered: "What are you saying? How can we stop our affair now? It's not right. I definitely won't break this relationship." He embraced her even tighter than before and kissed her passionately. Neither of them noticed that at that moment Pasang Yangki had arrived on the front doorstep.

Although Pasang Yangki had gone to attend the house-warming party of one of her colleagues, she had lost all her money and since she was feeling unhappy had decided to return home. As she opened the door and entered the house she saw the spectacle in the kitchen. For a moment, feeling stunned, she just stood where she was. But after a few seconds the colour in her face underwent a tremendous change. Tredön and Nyidröl hadn't yet noticed her and were kissing as if they were glued together. She collected herself and roared, "You criminals!" and then flung herself at them.

Apart from worrying that the children might see what they were doing, it hadn't occurred to them that Payang would arrive home so early. They were completely unprepared and in their astonishment remained frozen for a moment. It took them a few seconds to register what had happened. Payang pulled Nyidröl by her hair and scratched her face, behaving like a madwoman. When Tredön tried to stop her she grabbed the kitchen knife and tried to stab Tredön in the head. He snatched the knife from Payang's hand and struggled to push her to the floor. Nyidröl was still standing on the same spot, aghast, and it was only when Tredön said, "Aren't you going?" that she ran out crying. Payang broke all the bowls and thermos flasks in the kitchen. She rushed into the innermost room of the house and tried to smash other things there. Their neighbours, alarmed by the cacophony of things breaking and by the shouting, came running and stopped her. The two children were crying, completely terrified by the shouting; they squatted with a blanket wrapped around them. Payang was scolding and crying at the same time and Tredön was sitting on the sofa silently smoking a cigarette.

Pasang Yangki, sobbing, put on her clothes and jewellery, dressed the younger child and said, "Don't call me Pasang Yangki in case I don't separate from you from today on, you shameless man." However much the neighbours tried to stop her, she would not be deterred and left.

Outside it was raining gently and people returned to their own homes. Inside the house there was nobody left except Tredön and the elder child. There was silence. Tredön stroked his son's head and told him: "Son, you have to go to school tomorrow. Go to sleep." The child asked in a tremulous voice, "Where have my mother and sister gone?" Tredön said, "Your mother and your little sister have gone to Aca

Yudrön's home. They will come back tomorrow." At the same time he was wondering where Nyidröl had disappeared to.

Tredön remained on the bed, half lying down, and continued to draw on his cigarette. The smoke filled the home's interior until it was impossible to clearly discern what was there. It looked as if Tredön was thinking deeply, but at that moment there was no fixed thought in his head and, being free from thought, all the objects of his imagination had turned murky like the house filled with smoke.

Seven

After Pasang Yangki arrived at her friend Yudrön's, she spoke to her about her misery. She was crying and saying resolutely, "From now on there's no way I can live my life with him." That evening Yudrön entertained Payang and consoled her. She had some delicious *chang* and both of them drank till they were intoxicated. Next day Yudrön said, "You have two children and also a foundation of love. How would it be wise to divorce so suddenly? You left them alone like this as if you were purposely giving them an opportunity. If you stay away like this for a long time there is a great danger that you'll actually lose your husband to Nyidröl. The proverb says, 'Even though somebody is your sibling, your bellies are not siblings',[144] so it's not right to act impetuously. You should send Nyidröl away as soon as possible. Tredön will lose all hope and he will forget about her."

Though Pasang Yangki had suspected that the two of them were having an illicit affair, she did not have any proof. If she had raised the subject, it would have seemed that she suspected her own younger sister and in the eyes of her husband she would have appeared jealous of her own sibling. So she had not dared to speak about it. She thought that if some signs of danger had manifested earlier, the situation might not have developed to such an extent. She sighed in regret as she told this to her friend. The previous night, even though she had been intoxicated, her mind had been as clear as usual. She had not slept in the early hours of the morning and the more she thought about it she realised that if she divorced her husband she would have no other options for her future and, moreover, she saw that the children would be the ones to suffer most. She couldn't stand it, and since her friend was advising her like that she had to relinquish her previous firm decision. The more she considered it the more angry she felt at their behaviour. For a while she couldn't think of any sensible solution to the problem. She said to her friend, "They have disgraced themselves and her loss of good reputation is common knowledge. Who would want her?" She sighed deeply and looked forlorn. Yudrön reminded her, "Didn't Sithar ask to marry her?"

"Before, I did intend to give her to that man, but Nyidröl said that she would rather become a nun than be his wife. That shameless husband of mine didn't want to send her away. Now, even if she agreed to it, what would he say?"

Her friend replied, "Nyidröl's time to select a husband has gone now and other people will choose for her. However, as the saying goes, 'If you're hungry, even turnip root is delicious.' That man certainly needs a wife and hasn't managed to get one, so there's no need to fuss over that. So don't worry, my friend. I'll arrange it," and with that she promised to act as a go-between.

In the afternoon Yudrön led Pasang Yangki back to her home and with a commanding look told her husband that to act as he had was not at all the way to show true love but was irresponsible and would only harm Nyidröl's future. Now they should not allow the soiled water to run out on the road again, but should take care of themselves. She also spoke to Nyidröl, criticising and advising her. "Your illicit affair with Tredön does not demonstrate your affection for him. It amounts to snatching your sister's husband and destroying a family. Are you going to carry a stigma like that for the whole of your life?"

Tredön thought again and again and realised that while his heart was now attached to Nyidröl he and his wife had also chosen to love each other. Moreover, as they were connected by their children there was no way to divorce. He didn't wish to give up either of them. Usually people say that love acts from its own force and cannot be divided. However, when he thought about it he felt certain that he could share his love with both the sisters and the children and became convinced that they could all live together. But, that was not possible in real life and it was also something which Payang would not tolerate. And so, forced to choose, he decided that Nyidröl should be married.

Yudrön had gone to Sithar and said, teasingly, "Today I have come here with the intention of arranging a wife for you. Do you want one or not?"

Sithar replied in jest, "If it is you, I want her. If not, what's the use of other girls?"

To which Yudrön replied, emphatically: "I really mean it!"

"Now I have lost all hope of getting a wife, and isn't it better that an old man like me keeps happy eating his own food and doing his own work? Stop joking. Who is it?" Sithar ended hopefully.

Yudrön teased, "Look! When I mention a wife to you even your eyes get bigger!" Again she persisted, "You aren't a king's son. Why haven't you been more determined about winning Nyima Dölma?"

Sithar said, "I see. Is it Nyidröl?" For a while he rubbed his jaw and looked as if he was thinking. Yudrön said, "What? Is she no good? If you don't like it, nobody will force you." So saying, she started to get up. Sithar got anxious and to prevent her leaving said, "It's not like that. Not like that at all. Just stay. Why are you in such a hurry?" He continued, "I saw what was happening before. Still I jokingly told my friend that he should not think of keeping two. If she had been given to me, as Payang promised, everybody would be happy these days. Such a stupid thing has happened now." He looked sad.

Even though Yudrön understood what he was alluding to she acted as if she didn't and said, "I see. Now, when it's time to make a decision, you probably need someone completely pure and immaculate. Now I've got it!" And she stood up to go.

Sithar was horrified, "That's not it. Who could be more impatient than you? Does Nyima Dölma agree to this?" he asked.

Yudrön said, "It's all right. Just leave that to me." Sithar felt delighted and took some tins of drinks from the refrigerator and popped them in her bag. As he was doing that he patted her lightly on the buttocks, saying, "Then, I will trust you." and smiled.

Eight

When Nyidröl got to know that her elder sister and Tredön were going to give her to be Sithar's wife after all, she showed neither happiness nor sorrow and promised to do as they wished. Sithar again came carrying the marriage proposal *chang* and presents, asked Nyidröl to become his wife, and at the same time he gave her a pair of golden earrings to solemnise the engagement. Everything was peaceful as before and life continued so.

Nyidröl didn't want to go anywhere where there were lots of people and didn't want an elaborate marriage ceremony. Pasang Yangki and Tredön also expressed the hope that the ceremony would be arranged in a simple way. Not listening to them, Sithar said, "This is a great event in my life. Until now I have attended other people's respectable or wild parties and I owe them a grand party. You don't need to worry about the expenses." Now there was nothing for it so they had to keep busy with the preparations.

Though Tredön thought that he should take Nyidröl to one side and say some consoling words to her, Pasang Yangki had stopped playing mahjong and didn't leave them alone together for a moment. They couldn't even speak about everyday things and he certainly didn't get any opportunity for anything more.

Most of the preparations had been completed, and while they were arranging the cushions and tables Sithar called Payang to him to discuss the dishes to be served during the first day. The only people left in that big house were Tredön and Nyidröl, who were arranging the cushions and tables, and Tredön, while helping Nyidröl to shift a table, said, "Nyidröl, don't be angry. It was all my fault. I thought that it would be good to find a better husband than him..." Nyidröl's face, as ever, remained expressionless and she replied, "Nobody is to be blamed for that. It happened through the force of my actions in a previous life."

Tredön thought that Nyidröl was angry with herself and he felt very uncomfortable. In a whisper he said, "Nyidröl, actually I don't want to send you away at all. It's true but if I tell you that, you won't believe me." When he said that, Nyidröl's eyes suddenly filled with tears and with an intense expression on her face she looked at him for some time. Then she lowered her head, and said, "I believe it. I believe it. I also don't want to go to anyone else. However, two fingers won't fit into a single ring. It is all because of the force of our previous actions. Beginning from tomorrow, someone else will own me. When I have gone, you and the children will be the most unhappy ones. However, as my sister has now vowed not to play mahjong, probably nothing of the sort will happen again..." As she was saying this, Payang came in from outside shouting, "Tredön-la, haven't you finished yet?" And immediately after that she entered the house. While Nyidröl was speaking, Tredön was so moved that he was choking and a strong urge came over him to hold both her hands tightly. As he stretched out his hands his wife came in, and so he could do nothing. Nyidröl immediately vanished from her sister's sight and went into the toilet. Pasang Yangki sensed what was happening immediately, and as she noticed that Nyidröl was crying she got furious. She tried to suppress it as best as she could and went over to Tredön. Although she lowered her voice, her tone was incensed. "Thüü! You spoiled pig. You're shameless! I was thinking just that." She spat in his face, turned round, and went after Nyidröl.

Nyidröl was wiping away her tears in the toilet. Because of her anger, even Pasang Yangki's face had turned red and her body was shaking uncontrollably. She twisted Nyidröl's ear and attacked her. "You disgraceful, shameless creature! I thought that you had given up what you were doing before and would take some notice of the advice you've been given. You are so horrible. Since you now belong to another, be careful what you do and keep your heart under control. Otherwise, you'll regret it! Except for what is your *karma*, you cannot just do anything that comes into your head. Think about your situation." Nyidröl was shrieking and crying. Payang got alarmed and lowering her voice said: "Isn't it enough that you have brought about such disgrace? Aren't you going to shut your mouth?"

"Sister, you have everything. You have an office and a family. You have children. You have a salary. You have everything. Do I have to tell you what I am? When my parents were sending me to school, you promised them that you would do this and that for the good of my future. Now I've lost my reputation. I don't have any way to go. Do I have to say what I am? I'm being given as a wife to that kind of man. Should I say that he is my father or what should I say? What is there to see in him?" And she cried.

Pasang Yangki got frightened that others would hear the sound of crying and when she heard her younger sister's sad lament her anger almost died down. She said, "Now, don't cry. It will be horrible if other people hear you. As for life, it's impossible to get what you wish. You'll only get what is written as your *karma*. That is the same for everyone. Even if he is a bit older, that won't be a problem. Now please, don't cry." She also had tears in her eyes and Nyidröl stopped crying. Pasang Yangki made Nyidröl wash her face and said, "Since you have to leave tomorrow, go home early and wash your hair. There isn't much work left here. We'll take care of it." So she sent Nyidröl home ahead of time. For a few days the weather had been cloudy and each day seemed so dark. The trees lining both sides of the road were crowned with a thick canopy of leaves and the turquoise-coloured leaves cast an emerald green light. Nyidröl was walking along the side of the road with her head bent when suddenly she felt something light fall on her head. When she reached up for it and looked it was a yellow leaf. She felt surprised. But when she lifted her head and looked upwards she realised that it had fallen from a big tree by the roadside. Even though the entire tree was bent with the weight of its profusion of leaves, the sparse leaves growing on one thin branch had turned yellow. It made the whole tree look as if it was decorated with flowers. After seeing that she felt very sad and thought, "Why are there yellow leaves in this season?"

Nine

Next morning Pasang Yangki arose early, and noticing it was silent in the house she wondered why Nyidröl was not up yet. She put on the light and just as she was about to call her, she noticed that Nyidröl's blankets had been neatly folded and on top of them lay a pair of glittering golden earrings. Payang called, "Aunty! Aunty Nyidröl!" Nobody replied. Although she looked in the toilet and kitchen there was no sign of Nyidröl. Surprised and alarmed, she went out of the door and called "Nyidröl! Nyidröl!" Even though she shouted a few times, nobody answered. Pasang Yangki went quickly back into the house and, frightened, called, "Tredön-la! Tredön-la! Get up quickly! Sithar's Nyidröl isn't here. Come quickly!"

Tredön got up immediately and since the older child had also heard the shouting, he got out of bed and asked, "Where has Aunty gone?" Payang told him: "Son, as it's time for you to go to school, get up." She continued, alarmed, scolding her husband, "You've caused all this trouble. Now where has she gone?" Both spouses searched everywhere in the neighbourhood. They even looked at the bus station, but they didn't find her.

Although they were reluctant to ask others about her, they had no choice since they had to explain to Sithar. So Tredön continued searching in all the likely places and questioned people while Payang visited Sithar to tell him what had happened. When Sithar understood the situation he was so shocked that he couldn't say a thing. After a while he cried out, "If she had been a good girl how could she have been available for me? Now even my earrings have been pawned. She has made me a beggar. Only the Three Jewels know! What kind of bad *karma* did I commit in my previous life that this is the ripening result?"

When Pasang Yangki heard him saying this, even though she had thought of telling him that the golden earrings had been left behind, his words incensed her. So she only muttered "Hmm!" and left without saying anything more.

That day, though they searched everywhere they couldn't find her. Pasang Yangki cried uncontrollably. Grief-stricken she admitted, "I didn't handle this very well. Now it's the rainy season and it's raining heavily. If something tragic has happened to Nyidröl, what shall I say to our parents?"

Although Tredön thought of all the possible places where Nyidröl might have gone, he couldn't focus on any particular place. He said to his wife, "Don't get frightened too early. It's not possible that Nyidröl would do anything like that. Maybe she's gone back home?" Tears pouring, Payang said, "Nyidröl is proud and she wouldn't go back home in such a state. The reason why I'm worried is because of her pride. She may have done something reckless."

Tredön suddenly said: "Now I understand. Didn't Nyidröl say before that she would rather become a nun than get married to Sithar?"

Pasang Yangki said, "Then, shouldn't we first go to get a divination done?"

To which Tredön replied, "Oh yes. It's better to ask for a divination first."

"Where should we go for it?" asked Payang.

"What the goddess predicts will be accurate," said Tredön.

Hesitantly, they went together to the temple of the goddess to request divine guidance.

Written in Lhasa in November-December 1995.[145]

Notes

1. Although there are some Tibetan women writers though apparently not so numerous as men, the reason why I did not include any of their writings is that I was unable to locate a fascinating story portraying the fate of some female character written originally in Tibetan and also, even if I found some story written by a woman, judging from the name of the author, mostly it was difficult to find biographical information on the author or locate their other literary works. However, there are some women writers, for instance, in 1996 appeared in *sBrang char* dByangs sgrol's story entitled *"Sras mo g. Yang skyid sgrol ma"* ("Daughter Yangki Dölma") which is said to be excerpted from a novel entitled *"Lha ma ning"*; however, it bears a note that it was translated by g.Yung drung, thus it seems to have been originally written in Chinese. On the inside backcover of the same issue of *sBrang char* there is some information on dByangs sgrol and her other works. She is said to have been born in Lhasa in 1963 and since 1994 has worked in Beijing in the Research Centre of Tibetan Education of the PRC.

    Recently, after I had already completed the translations, appeared two new titles by women writing in Tibetan in exile, namely Chu skyes sGrol ma's *sPrin bral zla ba'i 'dzum rlabs* ("The Smile of A Cloudless Moon"), which contains mainly poetry and sKal bzang Lha mo's *Drang srong bsti gnas kyi rmi lam yun cig* (*Dreaming at the Sage's Abode: Biographical Sketches of Four Living Tibetan Nuns*). Although based on the life stories of real nuns, it is very different from traditional autobiography in its approach and the biographical sketches appear somewhat like short stories with passages of poetry inserted inside the narration.

2. See for instance Klu 'bum Ye shes rGya mtsho's *Zang zing gi 'jig rten* ("The World of Turmoil"), Klu smyon Ye shes rGya mtsho's (Klu 'bum and Klu smyon refer both to the same person) *Sham bha la'i dud sprin* ("The Clouds of Shambhala"), Gangs bzhad's *Gangs seng 'tshol du phyin pa* ("In Search of the Snow Lion"), dPal ldan rGyal's *mChod* ("Offering"), *Rang dbang* ("Freedom"), which contains contributions on the theme of 'freedom' by participants in the first International Conference of Tibetan Writers held in 1995 in Dharamsala, Be ri 'Jigs med dBang rgyal's *Dus rabs gsar pa'i rtsom rig pa zhig gi snying khams nas 'phos pa'i zungs khrag* ("The Blood Coming from the Heart of a Writer of the New Generation") and Chu skyes sGrol ma's *Sprin bral zla ba'i 'dzum rlabs* ("The Smile of a Cloudless Moon"). Some of the literary magazines are *rTsam pa* ("Tsampa") published by Tsampa Literature

Group, Sarah; *lJang gzhon* ("Young Green") from Amnye Machen Institute, Dharamsala; *lDum ra* ("Garden") from Dre-Gomang Buddhist Cultural Association, Mundgod; *Blo gsal rtsom rig dga' tshal* ("Losel Amusement Park of Literature") from Drepung Loseling Monastery, Mundgod; *Gangs ri'i lang tsho* ("The Youth of the Snow Mountains") from the Tibetan Medical and Astro Institute, Dharamsala and *Nor 'od* ("Jewel Light"), *Nor lde* ("Jewel Key") and *Nor rgyun* ("A Stream of Jewels") from the Norbulingka Institute, Sidhpur.

3. For information on a wide range of Tibetan language publications in the People's Republic of China, see Heather Stoddard, "Tibetan Publications and National Identity".

4. See 'Gyur med (ed.) *Lho yi dri bzhon* ("The South Wind").

5. A.A. Moon, "Modern Tibetan Fiction".

6. Heather Stoddard, "Don grub Rgyal (1953-1985): Suicide of a Modern Tibetan Writer and Scholar".

7. Mark Stevenson, "Paths and Progress: Some Thoughts on Don grub rgyal's 'A Threadlike Path'", and Rang grol (Don grub rgyal), trans. Mark Stevenson & Lama Choedak T. Yuthok, "A Threadlike Path".

8. Pema Bhum, trans. Lauran Hartley, "The Life of Dhondup Gyal: A Shooting Star that Cleaved the Night Sky and Vanished."

9. Pema Bhum, trans. Ronald Schwartz, "The Heart-beat of a New Generation: A Discussion of the New Poetry".

10. See p.338 and fn.2 in Alice Grünfelder, "Tashi Dawa and Modern Tibetan Literature".

11. See Pema Tsering, trans. Riika Virtanen, "The Deceitfully Erected Stone Pillar and the Beginnings of Modern Tibetan Literature" and Dexter Roberts' review of Tashi Dawa's *Soul in Bondage* entitled "Are You Tibetan or Chinese?".

12. Tashi Dawa, *A Soul in Bondage: Stories from Tibet* (for review, see D. Roberts, *op.cit.*).

13. For reference to it, see Heather Stoddard, "Don grub Rgyal ...", p.829.

14. See for example his short story "*Sog rus las mched pa'i rnam shes*" ("Consciousness Coming from a Shoulder Bone").

15. For a discussion of stylistic variation in modern Tibetan literature, with references to literary works, see Pema Tsering, trans. R. Virtanen, *op.cit.*

16. See p.50 in Rang grol, "*rTsom rig sgyu rtsal gyi snang brnyan skor cung tsam gleng ba*" ("A Short Discussion on Literary Images"). *rTsom rig sgyu rtsal gyi snang brnyan zer ba de 'tsho ba dngos kyi 'dra bshus tsam dang/ ri mo mkhan gyis mi zhig gi gzugs kyi cha byad ji ma ji bzhin du bris pa lta bu zhig e yin zhe na/ de'ang ma yin/... ...mi'i snang brnyan ni phyogs thams cad kyi snying po dang legs cha rnams bsdus nas byung ba zhig yin la/ rtsom pa pos rtsom yig gi brjod bya dang dgos pa nges can zhig la gzhigs nas gsar du bskrun pa zhig yin no//*

17. See p.83 in bKra shis dPal ldan, "*Don grub rgyal gyi brtsams 'bras dang des bod rigs kyi rtsom rig gsar par thebs pa'i shugs rkyen skor*" ("Don grub rGyal's Writings and Their Influence on Modern Tibetan Literature").

18. However, it should not be regarded as "the first modern Tibetan novel"; according to the message of congratulation by Krung go rtsom pa po'i mthun tshogs mtsho sngon yan lag mthun tshogs, in *sBrang char*, 1991, (1), p.9, the first Tibetan full-length novel is said to be rDo rje Tshe brtan's *Zhogs pa'i skya rengs slar yang shar dus* ("When the Dawn Rises Again") published by Mi dmangs rtsom rig dpe skrun khang. According to H. Stoddard: "the first modern novel of any length is *sKal-bzang Me-tog* (*The Flowers of the Good Age*), which is by 'Jam-dbyangs rGya-mtsho ...," H. Stoddard, "Tibetan Publications and National Identity," p.144. Also Don grub rGyal himself had already, before the appearance of *Sad kyis bcom pa'i me tog*, published several stories, among them "*sPrul sku*" ("Incarnation"). This is of considerable length (forty pages in the Amnye Machen edition) containing ten chapters. He also gained a prize in 1982 in the "First National Competition (*dpyad bsdur*) of Modern Literature of Minorities" for his composition "*Mi rtag sgyu ma'i rmi lam*" ("Impermanent Illusory Dream"), though this work was only published posthumously in 1986.

19. In Western contributions this work has been mentioned briefly by A.A. Moon who also provides a translation of a passage from it on p.20 of the first part of his article "Modern Tibetan Fiction". He has classified the story into a genre he calls "the genre of love and marriage". Also the story is mentioned in Pad ma 'Bum's "*Don grub rgyal gyi mi tshe*" on p.26, where it says that it and a few other of Don grub rGyal's stories which were published in *sBrang char* were like "rain in a time of drought for editors and readers".

20. See Ibid., pp.11-13.

21. *mi rigs skad yig 'dzin grwa.*

22. See Don grub rgyal, *dPal don grub rgyal gyi gsung 'bum* ("The Collected Works of Döndrub Gyel") Vol.1, Preface, p.1. The name of his degree is given as *hru'o hri* and according to Melvyn C. Goldstein's *Tibetan—English Dictionary of Modern Tibetan*, p.1222 this refers to M.A. or M.S. degree.

23. See Padma 'Bum, *op. cit.*, p.30 ff.

24. For more general information on these periods see chapters 13 and 14 ("The Great Proletarian Cultural Revolution in Tibet" and "Revival of Tibetan Nationalism") in Warren W. Smith, *Tibetan Nation*.

25. For some information on the contents of this book, see H. Stoddard, "Don grub Rgyal (1953-1985)", p.827.

26. For bibliographical information on his writings, see "*lJags rtsom gyi ming gzhung*" ("List of Writings" in pp.47-53 of Don grub rgyal, *Don grub rgyal gyi lang tsho'i rbab chu dang ljags rtsom bdams sgrig* ("Waterfall of Youth and Selected Writings of Don grub rGyal").

27. See Pema Bum, *op. cit.*, p.19 for a discussion of this pen-name.

28. For more information on modern free-style poetry in Tibet, see Padma 'Bum, *Mi rabs gsar pa'i snying khams kyi 'phar lding* ("The Heart Beat of the New Generation"). It also has as its appendix several modern poems, including the

"Waterfall of Youth", reprinted from originals published earlier in Tibet. For Döndrub Gyel's other poems, some written in the traditional style, some in free-style, see Vol.2 *sNyan ngag phyogs bsgrigs* ("Collected Poems") of his *gSung 'bum*.

29. In the list of Don grub rGyal's writings *"lJags rtsom gyi ming gzhung"* compiled by A.A. Moon in pp.47-53, *op.cit.*, mention is made of two reprints; on pp.316-398 of 'Gyur med (ed.), *rTa nag sgrog 'gros* ("The Galloping of a Black Horse") (Bod kyi deng rabs rtsom rig dpe tshogs), mTsho sngon mi rigs dpe skrun khang, 1991/2 and on p.27 f. of Ngag dbang Phun tshogs (ed.) *Don grub rgyal gyi brtsams sgrung phyogs bsgrigs* ("Anthology of Döndrub Gyel's Writings"), Mi rigs dpe skrun khang 1990/6.

30. For a translation of *"rKang lam phra mo"* see Rang grol, trans. M. Stevenson & Lama Choedak T. Yuthok, *op. cit.*

31. Don grub rGyal, *Don grub rgyal gyi lang tsho'i rbab chu dang ljags rtsom bdams sgrig*.

32. See Don grub rGyal, *dPal don grub rgyal gyi gsung 'bum* ("The Collected Works of Döndrub Gyel"), Vol.2 *brTsams sgrung phyogs bsgrigs* ("The Collected Stories"), pp.218-288.

33. In an article called *"rTsom rig gi kun ral dus rabs kyi 'phar rtsa"* ("The Garden of Literature—The Pulse of the Century"), pp.1-3, Don grub dBang 'bum states that the basic objective and aim of literature is to show affection for the common masses by rendering one's service to them through literary works.

34. The Chinese word *zawen* means "prose" or "prose essay in modern colloquial style".

35. See M. Stevenson, *op.cit.*, pp.58-59.

36. Rang grol, *"rTsom rig sgyu rtsal gyi snang brnyan skor cung tsam gleng ba,"* p.50. *"mi'i phyi mo yang de dang 'dra bar bsam bzhin du mi gcig bkol ba ni med par/ nam yin kyang kha ni kre cang dang/ gdong ni pe cin/ gos ni hran zhis nas blangs te de rnams bsdu bsgrig byas pa zhig yin."*

37. Their names are given as "Ko er ci" and "Pā er kra khi". Jane Perkins and Michael Futrell suggested that these probably refer to Maxim Gorki and Balzac.

38. See Don grub rGyal, *dPal don grub rgyal gyi gsung 'bum*, Vol.4, *bsGyur rtsom phyogs bsgrigs* ("Collected Translations"). In connection with the translations no information has been provided on the authors of the works Döndrub Gyel translated, only their names being provided in Tibetan script. Being not familiar with these writers I could only infer the source language being Chinese on the basis of Chinese appearing spellings, though some of the stories translated were clearly located in Tibet. Two of his translations trace to Indian origins, namely a part of *"Bya len ma'i zlos gar"* ("The Drama of Jalenma") and a part of the first chapter of *"Rā ma ṇa'i rtogs brjod"* ("Rāmāyaṇ").

39. Oral information from Pema Tsering, DIIR, 18.10.1997.

40. This is in contrast with, for example, bKra shis Zla ba's *"Bod ljongs/ rgyun bu'i mdud pa la brgyus pa'i rnam shes"* ("Tibet—A Consciousness Knotted in a

Leather Strap") p.314, where in the description of a landscape there is mention of its resemblance to a painting by Salvador Dali. Also some modern Tibetan authors do not necessarily set their stories in Tibet. For instance, "*Nu bo sprul skur ngos bzung rjes*" ("After the Recognition of My Younger Brother as an Incarnated Lama"), written by 'Jigs med 'Phel rgyas, is located largely in Beijing. However, it seems to have been written originally in Chinese, as at the end of the story it says: "Selected from *Bod kyi rtsom rig* and translated by bSam 'phel" (*Bod kyi rtsom rig* appears also in a Chinese edition).

41. I opted for the shorter way of translating the title, though it leaves out the "frost". But as it sounds better and as most flowers in the cold region of the Tibetan plateau could be assumed to be blighted due to frost, I thought this abbreviation of the title to be well-grounded.

42. See my translation of "Here Also is a Living Heart Strongly Beating" in Appendix A.

43. See p.3 in Don grub dBang 'bum, *op. cit.*

44. See Rang grol, trans. M. Stevenson and Lama Choedak T. Yuthok, *op. cit.* and Na ga Sangs rgyas bsTan dar, "*rKang lam phra mo la gzhi bcol te gzhung lam chen mor bgrod dgos pa*" ("The Necessity of Proceeding to the Great Avenue Basing Oneself on the Narrow Footpath").

45. See for instance, bKra shis Zla ba, "*gTsang po'i pha rol na*" ("On the Other Side of the River"); Don grub rGyal "*'Brong stag thang*" ("The Plain of Wild Yak and Tiger"); bKra shis dPal ldan, "*gNyan sgrig*" ("Marriage"); for an exile story in which an arranged marriage leads to suicide see Chab 'gag 'Jam mgon "*sKyo snang gi zlos gar*" ("Melancholic Opera Performance").

46. For a description of the power of the "marriage certificate" see Tshe ring Don grub, "*Ra lo*". In one situation the wife of the main character called Ralo is taken by another man and rightfully claimed by him as they have obtained a "marriage certificate". In the other situation the main character obtains a "marriage certificate" with the wife of another man he has just met. However, in the end, his new wife has to suffer six months imprisonment as she is found guilty of obtaining two marriage certificates.

47. Dr. Hubert Decleer pointed out to me that writers who end up taking their own life often have a scene depicting a suicide or some hint of it in their production. Oral communication in Chonor House, Dharamsala 16.9.1997.

48. See Pad ma 'Bum, *op. cit.*, p.39 and Lauran Hartley's translation of it "The Life of Dhondup Gyal", p.26, which corrects the date of the disagreement to 29th November, after consultation with the author.

49. See Ibid., pp.41-42 and p.27 in Lauran Hartley's translation.

50. Heather Stoddard, "Don grub Rgyal (1953-1985)", p.826.

51. Oral information from Pema Tsering in a discussion during autumn 1997.

52. Reprinted in pp.97-101 of Don grub rGyal, *Don grub rgyal gyi lang tsho'i rbab chu dang ljags rtsom bdams sgrig.*

53. Don grub rGyal, "*'Di na'ang drag tu mchongs lding byed bzhin pa'i snying gson po zhig 'dug*", p.100. Afterwards, I noticed that these same lines have also been quoted by rNga ba Tshe rgyam while discussing the characteristics of Tibetan poetry in p.8 of his article "*rTsom rig dang 'brel ba'i bod kyi snyan ngag gi skor rob tsam gleng ba*" ("A Short Discussion on Tibetan Poetry—A Literary Art").

54. The "List of Writings" in Don grub rGyal, "*Don grub rgyal gyi lang tsho'i rbab chu...*", p.50 indicates that it was reprinted on pp.82-103 of a publication called *gSar bzhad me tog tshom bu*, ("*Newly Blossoming Bunch of Flowers*") edited by mGon po Dar rgyas and published by Mi rigs dpe skrun khang 1990 (8).

55. There are many places called Brag dkar in Tibet, at least in sTod and Khams, but in this story it probably refers to the place in sPre'u district (*rdzong*) in the region south of Amdo's Blue Lake (mTsho lho). Oral information from Sonam Wangyel 1.6.1998 LTWA.

56. Ibid., p.78. *sgrung gi brjod bya gtso bo ni spyi tshogs ring lugs kyi khyim tshang gsar ba dang khyim gyi spyod lam ji ltar 'dzugs pa de red.*

57. Ibid., p.78. *khyim gyi spyod lam ni spyi tshogs ring lugs kun spyod kyi nang gi gal che shos shig yin pas/ bde skyid ldan pa'i khyim tshang zhig yin na mi'i blo sems bde zhing snying stobs rgyas pa dang/ gzhan la skul spel byas nas yar thon gong 'phel yong ba zhig yin/*

58. The *Tibetan-English Dictionary* of Chandra Das contains the following description of *glag*: "*glag* or *bya glag* a bird described as resembling an eagle, but smaller than the vulture and larger than the hawk, of blackish chocolate colour; carries away kids and lambs. This bird is numerous in Mongolia, Central Tibet and Kham. Probably the lammergayer" (p.254).

59. This kind of salt-expedition has also been documented in film in 1997, namely Ulrike Koch's "Die Salzmänner von Tibet" (Catpics Coproductions, Zürich). For its review, see Toni Huber's film review in *The Tibet Journal*, Vol.22, No.4, Winter 1997, pp.115-117.

60. Pages 62-88 and 89-115 respectively in *Byang thang gi mdzes ljongs.*

61. Ibid., pp.100-101.

62. I notice that placing himself in his fiction is not unique to this work; for example, at the beginning of his "*A ri'i shig*" ("An American Louse"), there is a brief remark about the main character borrowing money from "friend Tenpa Yargye".

63. See H. Stoddard, *op.cit.,* p.830.

64. According to H. Stoddard, *op.cit*, p.830, there is a collection of bKra shis dPal ldan's works called *Phyi nyin gnam gshis de ring las legs pa yong nges* ("Tomorrow the Weather Will Certainly Be Better than Today"), apparently published in a series called Bod kyi deng rabs rtsom pa po'i dpe tshogs. It is possible to gain some idea of the title-story from sGrol skyid's article titled "*re ba can gyi mi rigs dang khong tsho'i rkang rjes—<<phyi nyin gyi gnam gshis*

de ring las legs pa yong nges>> zhes pa'i brtsams sgrung sgrung bklags rjes*", ("The People with Hopes and Their Foot-prints—After reading the story called 'Tomorrow the Weather Will Certainly Be Better than Today'".

65. Heather Stoddard (1994), refers to this article in p.830 of her paper, but she has read it as the last item of a collection of stories titled *Phyi nyin gnam gshis de ring las legs pa yong nge* ("The Weather will Certainly be Better Tomorrow").

66. Actually, TIN Briefing Paper No.31, 1999 *Social Evils: Prostitution and Pornography in Lhasa,* pp.6-7 reports that many girls from rural areas come to Lhasa to work as maids and in a statement by a now exiled Tibetan we find a situation resembling much of that described in Tashi Palden's story.

67. See bsTan pa Yar rgyas, *"mGo ras kyis btums pa'i bu mo"*, p.93.

68. *sder ka,* (or *sder kha*) an arrangement of *kha zas* (biscuits of deep-fried dough) piled in layers and decorated with sweets, fruits etc., which adorns Tibetan altars during Lo gsar—the Tibetan New Year—celebrations.

69. Tib. *phu bo.* The relevance of calling somebody "elder brother" is probably because a younger brother should show respect to the elder one and also, as found in the words of their father in the dialogue on p.26, the eldest of the brothers was normally the one whose responsibility it was to take care of the family property.

70. The Tibetan original, p.7, uses the word *a rgya,* explained in parentheses as the term for elder brother in the dialect of gCan tsha, an area of Amdo province located between Reb gong to the south and sKu 'bum in the north (see *Bod chol kha gsum gyi 'grim 'grul sa khra, Road Map of Tibet,* Research & Analysis Centre, CTA, 1994).

71. *blo pha la 'dri mi dgos pa dang bro ma la slong mi dgos pa,* a proverb for reaching the age of independence.

72. *mag pa,* custom of a groom moving to the bride's family home; usually to a family with no male heir.

73. Literally, to bite one's teeth (*so*) against one's jaw (*ma kha*).

74. *gSer mo ljongs,* "Golden Area", is another name for Reb gong.

75. *a ga ru,* eaglewood or aloewood, *Aquilaria agallocha.* According to Dr. Barry Clark's *The Quintessence Tantras of Tibetan Medicine,* p.140, there are two types of this wood, black and yellow, and they respectively have bright blue and pale blue flowers.

76. The actual expression used is *phyogs bzhi mtshams brgyad* which translated literally says "four directions and eight intermediary directions".

77. *rtswa pad ma* is a type of flower growing in Tibet, but in contrast to actual lotus which grows in water, it grows on land. There are said to be three kinds of lotuses: 1) those that grow in water 2) *rtswa pad ma* and 3) *shing pad ma,* which bloom on trees (oral information from Pema Tsering at DIIR).

78. *mo sgo mdzes po* refers to beautiful or handsome looks in A mdo dialect; the central dialect (*dbus skad*) would use *rnam pa mdzes po.*

79. These days the word for *kung hre,* here translated as commune, is *zhang;* the various villages (*grong tsho/sde pa*) of an area are under one *kung hre.*
80. *sle bo* is a woven basket slung over the shoulders.
81. Lit. 'outstretched wings of a vulture'.
82. *ke ta ka,* Skt., *ketaka,* Das: "1. a gem which has the property of purifying water" (p.30).
83. *'tshams rtags* is a significant present sent by boys or girls to the opposite sex to whom they are attracted. In this story a ring and a scarf filled with sweets are examples of *'tshams rtags* gifts.
84. Seng lcam 'brug mo was King Ge sar's beautiful queen, who was abducted by the King of Hor, Gur dkar rgyal po, and then freed by Ge sar. To learn more about her, see the following English translations of the Gesar epic: Alexandra David Neel & Lama Yongden, *The Superhuman Life of Gesar of Ling* and Douglas J. Penick, *The Warrior Song of King Gesar.*
85. Yid 'phrog lha mo was the beautiful Gandharva girl who married Prince Nor bzang in *Chos rgyal nor bzang gi rnam thar* ("The Life Story of Dharma King Nor bzang"). See *Chos kyi rgyal po nor bu bzang po'i rnam thar phyogs bsgrigs byas pa thos chung yid kyi dga' ston* ("The Compiled Life Story of the Religious King Nor bu bZang po—The Celebration for the Minds of the Uneducated"). For English abridged translations of this story, refer to Joanna Ross, *Lhamo: Opera from the Roof of the World,* pp.91-96 and Wang Yao, *Tales from Tibetan Opera,* pp.42-72 which presents a slightly more extensive version.
86. Gling dkar stod refers to a region mentioned in Ge sar legends.
87. *ma dgos na rgya sgo/ ma byin na myi kha/.* My informant from Amdo explained this saying that there used to be a lot of Chinese beggars coming from areas bordering Amdo.
88. *mig zhags* is literally translated as "look of a lasso", lasso-like look.
89. The text has here (p.19) the following footnote numbered as n.1, explaining the meaning of the interjection used, Tib. *ma:* "An indication of giving a thing away in the A mdo dialect."
90. The text (p.21) has *snying langs pa zhig la* which the footnote explains has a connotation in the A mdo dialect of *khros pa;* "being angry".
91. The text has *ru rta* with a footnote explaining that in the A mdo dialect this has the meaning of *rtsa ba;* "root", "basis".
92. Literally it says (p.21): *brdzun gyi rnga ma skyong ba;* "taking care of the tail of the lie."
93. *slong chang,* the "beer for requesting the bride's hand" refers to the custom of taking a present of beer to the girl's family. Even other presents can be presented to the family before that, it is considered that after presenting the *slong chang* there should not be any change of the decision to give her as bride. For marriage customs in Tibet, see P.W. Barshi's *gNa' rabs bod kyi chang sa'i lam srol* (*Tibetan Marriage Custom,* see especially pp.3-6 for the presents and *slong chang* presented on deciding upon the marriage) and Lobsang Shastri's "The Marriage

Customs of Ru-thog (Mnga'-ris)" which mentions on p.759 the *gros chang* "wine for discussion" and also refers (note 10) to the above-mentioned title on the custom of presenting the *slong chang.*

94. *kha nag,* which has here been translated literally, has the meaning of someone who speaks inauspicious things which bring harm to others.

95. *chang* is Tibetan beer brewed from fermented barley grains.

96. Bla brang is located to the south-east of Reb gong and sKu 'bum.

97. *maṇi*-mantra, the six-syllable mantra of Avalokiteśvara: *oṃ maṇi padme huṃ.*

98. *spyi tshogs rnying pa,* 'old society' refers to Tibet before the 1950s and the Chinese Communist invasion.

99. 1950, the year the People's Liberation Army invaded and "liberated" Tibet.

100. *sgo gsum,* lit. 'three doors'. Our actions can be divided into three categories: physical, verbal and mental actions. In this context "respects through the three doors" would be performing prostrations of the body, paying verbal homage by reciting prayers and maintaining respectful mental attitude.

101. *'then thug,* a Tibetan pasta soup.

102. This refers to a legend of Buddha's earlier births as a *bodhisattva* when he incarnated as a rabbit. The legend relates how the rabbit jumped into flames and offered his body as a meal to a brahmin, an embodiment of Indra. To honour this supreme act of generosity to benefit the beings of this world, Indra ornamented the moon with an image of a rabbit. See the sixth chapter on taking birth as a rabbit in 'Phags pa dpa' bo, *sKyes pa'i rabs kyi rgyud* (*Jātaka-mālā*), ff.18a^8-22a^3 or pp.37-45 in J.S. Speyer, *The Jātakamālā: Garland of Birth-Stories of Āryaśūra,* which contains an English translation of the story based on the Sanskrit original.

103. Three Jewels (*dkon mchog gsum*; Sans. *triratna*) refers to the three objects of Buddhist refuge-taking: Buddha, dharma and sangha.

104. *mgo mi chud sar lus btsangs.* This idiomatic expression suggests getting involved with something one should have nothing to do with and have no experience in. In this context it refers to an ordained person getting involved with matters related to worldly love affairs.

105. Myang tsha dkar rgyan was the name of Mi la ras pa's mother. For her sufferings see the second chapter of Rus pa'i rgyan can's *rNal 'byor gyi dbang phyug chen po mi la ras pa'i rnam mgur* ("The Life Story and Songs of the Great Yogi Mi la ras pa") or pp.17-21 in Lobsang P. Lhalungpa, *The Life of Milarepa.*

106. rGan gya is located in the area of Bla brang.

107. Ma Bufang, the Hui governor of Sining, who demanded a large ransom from the Tibetan government for allowing His Holiness the 14th Dalai Lama to journey from his birthplace sTag 'tsher to Lhasa. See Dalai Lama, *My Land and My People,* pp.25-28 and Warren W. Smith, *Tibetan Nation,* p.241.

108. *dge bsnyen ma'i sdom pa,* lay-ordination; the five vows of an *upāsikā* consist of vowing to refrain from killing, stealing, sexual misconduct, lying and taking intoxicants.

109. The Tibetan original is a proverb which I have rendered in a more free manner to interpret its implicit meaning: *kha khog pas ma gsang\ glo rgyu mas ma bskums* would literally translate as "heart not hidden from the mouth" and "the intestines not pressing the lungs".
110. To say one thing but mean another.
111. Literally: 'the eighteen facts and twenty ways', *gnas lugs bco brgyad dang yin lugs nyi shu.*
112. Kun mkhyen 'Jam dbyangs bZhad pa Ngag dbang brTson 'grus (1648-1721 AD) was the founder of Labrang bKra shis 'khyil monastery. See mKhas btsun bZang po, *Biographical Dictionary of Tibet and Tibetan Buddhism,* Vol.V, pp.650-660.
113. *damaruḥ,* a small double-sided handdrum, used during ritual.
114. Lit. 'turquoise mane' (*g.yu ral*). The snow lion (*gangs seng*)—mythical protector of Tibet—is depicted as white with a turquoise blue mane and tail. For a discussion on snow lion—or rather on its non-existence—refer to dGe 'dun Chos 'phel's *Ri bo hi ma la'i bstan bcos* ("A Treatise of the Himalaya Mountains"), which has been translated into English by Thupten K. Rikey and will appear in *The Tibet Journal,* Vol.25, No.4, Winter 2000 (forthcoming).
115. In Das's *Tibetan-English Dictionary,* p.463, two species of *'jol mo* are described: "*'jol nag* said to be a species of blackbird identical with *Merula ruficollis,* and *'jol khra* a middle-sized piebald bird described as white in colour with yellow markings and with a daub of red behind each ear."
116. *bsam blo bzhi gsum bcu gnyis;* literally, "twelve thoughts".
117. The original text, part II, p.23, has sobs between the phrases transliterated as *'ang 'ang 'un/ he hi* and so on, which I chose not to include in the translation.
118. The *sBrang char* edition has in the beginning of Wangtsho's words the syllable *tho,* of which meaning I could not find out. However, the *gSung 'bum* of Döndrub Gyel, Vol.2 (*brtsams sgrung phyogs bsgrigs,* "Collected Stories"), p.280 has the syllable *bo,* which seems to have the meaning of 'old man'.
119. *zhwa mo rna bzhi* is an embroidered Tibetan traditional hat, which has "extensions" on its four sides.
120. Here the spelling of the name differs slightly from the Jili Lhündrub (*Byis li Lhun grub*) who was mentioned before, but probably the same character is meant anyway.
121. *sna lo.*
122. When the tea is not standard Tibetan butter tea, and is mere black tea, Tibetans add a small piece of butter in each cup for a buttery flavor.
123. Lit. "due to her years and months"; *lo dang nam zla'i dbang gis.*
124. The text has *skyid,* but probably in this context it is a mis-spelling for *skyin.*
125. A special method of cleaning kitchen utensils.
126. *pho 'dom* actually means a distance of out-stretched arms, and one *pho 'dom* has been approximated to be about two yards.

127. This expression is rendered in a somewhat free manner trying to catch something of the tone of the actual expression in the nomad dialect, which reads *g.ye byed rgyu/ shi thal ye/*

128. *rgyang grags,* Das, p.307: "(Skt.) *krośa,* the distance of about two miles; the reach of hearing."

129. *shang* is explained as follows in the Glossary of Victoria Conner's and Robert Barnett's *Leaders in Tibet:* "*xiang* (Chinese)—township. The lower level administrative unit, formerly covering a township, but in rural areas covering a group of villages. Tibetan: *shang* (p.xiv)."

130. This refers to the objects of Buddhist refuge-taking, the Three Jewels (*dkon mchog gsum*), which are Buddha, dharma and sangha.

131. *Krung go'i par rgyag.*

132. *Bod ljongs brnyan par.*

133. *Byang thang mdzes ljongs.*

134. The text has actually *gos 'khru 'phrul 'khor,* lit. "washing machine".

135. *gangs lha me tog,* I have here translated the name of this flower literally as a "snow-goddess" flower, as I could not find the actual English or Latin name of this species of flower.

136. *Mi rigs brnyan par.*

137. *khru,* a measure of the length from one's elbow to the fingertips.

138. *'dom,* a measurement indicating the length between the out-stretched arms of a person.

139. *spags* denotes a staple Tibetan dish of roasted barley flour (*rtsam pa*) mixed with a liquid, such as tea, and moulded with ones hands into bite-size balls while eating.

140. See before n.129.

141. See before n.93.

142. Ge sar was the legendary, heroic king of gLing.

143. Tredön is the abbreviation of the full name Tashi Döndrub. Taking the first syllables of both names to form an abbreviated name is a common practice among Tibetans. This story also has Nyidröl for Nyima Dölma and Payang for Pasang Yangki.

144. *bu spun yin yang grod pa spun min.* This proverb has the implied meaning: "personal life is separate".

145. At the end of the story on p.48 of the Tibetan original it is mentioned that this story was edited by Chung bdag.

146. This poem was first published in *mTsho sngon mang tshogs sgyu rtsal,* 1986, no.1. The translation is based on the edition published by Amnye Machen Institute in Don grub rgyal, *Don grub rgyal gyi lang tsho'i rbab chu dang ljags rtsom bdams sgrig,* pp.97-101. The present translation is quite a rough, literal translation of the poem to give some idea of its contents, as I found it difficult to capture the original poetic beauty in another language. I have tried to a large extent to preserve the author's spacing though sometimes I was compelled

to change the order of lines due to different word-order of Tibetan and English or divide a longer sentence into several lines. A native English poet might restructure the poem differently, but in taking more freedom, I feared that some of the original sense might get lost. To enjoy the actual poetic flavour and beauty of this poem, the reader should refer to the Tibetan original.

147. *bka' bstan* refers to the Tibetan Buddhist Canon; i.e. *bka' 'gyur,* 'the translated words of the Buddha' and *bstan 'gyur,* 'the translations of their commentaries'.

148. *zhal lce dga' gsum dang 'dar gsum,* according to oral information from Acarya Sangye Tendar Naga, LTWA 5.6.1998, refer to some of the ancient Tibetan laws established by Srong btsan sGam po. I tried to find these laws mentioned in some of the *chos 'byung*s, but could not immediately locate them under this name, but for example in dMu dge bSam gtan's *Bod du rig gnas dar tshul mdor bsdus bshad pa* ("A Brief Explanation on the Spread of Learning in Tibet") p.12, where among "fifteen laws of the kingdom" (*rgyal khrims bco lnga*) the following groups of three laws are mentioned: *mdzad pa gsum* "three 'do's", *mi mdzad pa gsum* "three 'don'ts'", *bstod pa gsum* "three praiseworthy ones", *smad pa gsum* "three depreciable ones" and *mi mnar ba gsum* "three non-tormenting ones".

149. Please note that the "phonetic transliterations" are not always strictly phonetic, but many times in accordance with the normal usage of how Tibetans tend to spell their names, when they write them in the Latin alphabet.

APPENDIX A

Here Also is a Living Heart Strongly Beating[146]

Döndrub Gyel

Beauty
marvels
loveliness
Since the formation of the world
     fascinating events of history
     the beauty of the enchanting canonical works[147]
     the treasuries of knowledge difficult to forget
          how many of them have come into being!

Also this race of our own
has certainly been formed
from the aggregation of physical substances, flesh and blood
     sharp intelligence
     life-force of dignity
     volition of mental faculties
     the physical body ... ...
          rarely obtained ... ...
          with eight freedoms and ten riches ... ...
     the illusory dance of its union with consciousness
     subject and object
     means and wisdom
          based on them all
     a foundation for families originated
     in this land of moderate climate,
          isn't it so?

Really! As for our ancestors ... ...
          before the complete development
          of their capacities of verbal expression and understanding ... ...
the marvellous oral tradition
unfathomable to other races
of the bodhisattva monkey
and the rock-ogress—the emanation of wrathful Tārā,
and their descendants
          in solitary forests
          expansive meadows
          and desolate deserts
even during the age when leaves were worn as clothes,
                              certainly existed.
However, that is also a witness of history
          and a memorial of events past.
Oh, ... oh, friends,
          eating meat, doesn't make one a carnivore
          and how could all those with red-face
          be of the race of monkeys?
In times before also
          those red-faced meat eaters were known
          as the battle-force of Tibet
          the banner of their fame
          fluttered in the sky
          the fame of their heroic deeds ... ...
                    in the noble land of India
                    in the realm of the great land of China
... and ...
          in Nepal,
          Kashmir
          Sikkim
          Bhutan and other places ...
                    Did you notice how it resounded
                    like the melodies of clouds
                    sound of the guitar
                    the song of gandharvas
                    and the song of Sarasvatī?

However, to bring ...
>> a new way of thinking
>> a new view
>> a new way of believing
>> and a new custom
... to the Snowy Land with the socialist system ...
>> ... is like ...
>> the horn of a rhinoceros
>> the fur of a turtle
>> a lotus on the sky
>> and a rainbow on earth,
>> do you know how difficult it is?
It definitely is.
>> Even it seems that,
>> in this sphere of conservatism
>> the clouds of habitual patterns waver
>> the lightnings of lack of self-confidence flash,
>> and only tiny drops of the gentle rain of progress ripple.
But ...
>> the vapour of the hopes of the people will surely rise to the sky,
>> the blue cloud of the prestige of the Snowy Land will surely
>>> float from the south
>> and those who have wandered away and those staying,
>> the people inside Tibet and those in exile,
>> are about to rise up.
Do not despair,
>> young people,
Although it is true that in the mouth of people is an eye of wisdom,
but as three amicable laws and three fearsome laws exist,[148]
>> how could you despair?
Do not feel depressed
>> youth of the Snowy Land,
>>> if there is no power of creativity
>>> honesty and truth will not exist
>>> Also the law of cause and effect becomes a lie.

But ...

        what appears in my eyes... ...
             is the nectar of happiness
          and what resounds in my ears
             is the life of times to come.
This is ... the living heart
          strongly beating in my mind
This is ... the living heart
          strongly beating
             ... perhaps in your minds too ...

July 21, 1985

APPENDIX B

Names of Persons, Places etc. with their corresponding
transliteration in the Wylie system of transliteration

Phonetic[149] transliteration	Wylie transliteration
Agya Rigyag	A rgya Rig yag
Akhu Nyima	A khu Nyi ma
Akhu Sangye	A khu Sangs rgyas
Barkor	Bar skor
chuba	*phyu pa*
Chungdag	Chung bdag
Dargye	Dar rgyas
Dawa Tashi	Zla ba bkra shis
Dekyi	bDe skyid
Dölkar	sGrol dkar
Dölma Pelmo	sGrol ma dPal mo
Dorje	rDo rje
Dragkar Dzakang	Brag dkar rDza rkang
Dragkar Sermojong	Brag dkar gSer mo ljongs
Döndrub	Don grub
dzo	*mdzo*
Gengya	rGan gya
Gengye Tingring	rGan gya'i rting ring
Gesar	Ge sar
Gyali	rGya li
gyama	*rgya ma*
Jamyang Zhedpa Ngawang Tsöndrü	'Jam dbyangs bzhad pa Ngag dbang brtson 'grus
Jamyang Sherab	'Jam dbyangs shes rab

Jangthang	Byang thang
Jili Lhündrub	Byis li Lhun grub
jölmo	*'jol mo*
karma	*skar ma*
Kelbhe	sKal bhe
Kumbum	sKu 'bum
Küntu Sangmo	Kun tu bZang mo
Labrang	Bla brang
Labrang Tashi Khyil	Bla brang bKra shis 'khyil
Lacha	La cha
Lhachog	Lha mchog
Lhakyi	Lha skyid
Lhamo	Lha mo
Lhatsho	Lha mtsho
Lhe	Lhas
Lhündrub	Lhun grub
Lingkar Töd	Gling dkar stod
Losar	Lo gsar
Nachen	Na chen
Nagchu	Nag chu
Malho	rMa lho
Mön	Mon
Nyangtsha Kargyen	Myang tsha dkar rgyan
Nyidröl	Nyi sgrol
Nyima Dölma	Nyi ma sGrol ma
Pasang Yangki	Pa sangs dByangs skyid
Payang	Pa dbyangs
Phüntshog	Phun tshogs
Ralo	Ra lo
Rebkong Sermojong	Reb kong gSer mo ljongs
Rigpel	Rig dpal
Rigyag	Rig yag
Sangmo	bZang mo
Silin Lhündrub	Si lin Lhun grub
Sithar	Sri thar
Söbhe	bSod bhe
Tagnag	sTag nag

Tashi	bKra shis
Tashi Palden	bKra shis dPal ldan
Tashi Tshering	bKra shis Tshe ring
Tenpa Yargye	bsTan pa Yar rgyas
Tredön	bKras don
Tsheten Lhamo	Tshe brtan Lha mo
Tshomo	mTsho mo
Zöpa	bZod pa
Tashi Döndrub	bKra shis Don grub
Thrating	Khra ting
Thrika	Khri ka
Tongkhor	sTong 'khor
Tshelo	Tshe lo
Tshering	Tshe ring
Tshokyi	'Tsho skyid
Tsongchu	Tsong chu
Wangmo	dBang mo
Wangtsho	dBang mtsho
Yudrön	g.Yu sgron

Bibliography

Works in Western Languages

Barnett, Robert and Shirin Akiner (eds.), *Resistance and Reform in Tibet*, London: Hurst & Company, 1994.

Clark, Barry, *The Quintessence Tantras of Tibetan Medicine*, Ithaca: Snow Lion Publications, 1995.

Dalai Lama, *My Land and My People*, New York: Potala Corporation, 1977.

Das, Chandra, *Tibetan-English Dictionary*, Compact Edition, New Delhi: Gaurav Publishing House, 1991.

David-Neel, Alexandra & Lama Yongden, *The Superhuman Life of Gesar of Ling*, Boston: Shambhala, 1987.

Goldstein, Melvyn C., *Tibetan-English Dictionary of Modern Tibetan*, Kathmandu: Ratna Pustak Bhandar, 1975.

Conner, Victoria & Robert Barnett, *Leaders in Tibet: A Directory*, London: (T.I.N.) Tibet Information Network, 1997.

Grünfelder, Alice, "Tashi Dawa and Modern Tibetan Literature", in Ernst Steinkellner, *Tibetan Studies: Proceedings of the 7th Seminar of the International Association for Tibetan Studies, Graz 1995*, Vol.1, Verlag der Österreichischen Akademie der Wissenschaften, Wien, 1997, pp.337-345.

Lhalungpa, Lobsang P., *The Life of Milarepa*, Boston: Shambhala Publications, 1985.

Lobsang Shastri, "The Marriage Customs of Ru-thog (Mnga'-ris)" in Per Kvaerne (ed.) *Tibetan Studies, Proceedings of the 6th Seminar of the International Association for Tibetan Studies, Fagernes 1992*, Oslo: The Institute for Comparative Research in Human Culture, 1994, pp.755-767.

Moon, A.A., "Modern Tibetan Fiction", Part I, *Tibetan Review,* October 1991, pp.19-25; Part II, *Tibetan Review,* November 1991, pp.15-20 and Part III, *Tibetan Review,* December 1991, pp.13-17.

Pema Bhum, trans. Lauran Hartley, "The Life of Dhondup Gyal: A Shooting Star that Cleaved the Night Sky and Vanished", *Lungta,* (a special issue called *two thousand years & more of tibetan poetry*) No.9, Winter 1995, pp.17-29.

Pema Bhum, trans. Ronald Schwartz, "The Heart-beat of a New Generation: A Discussion of the New Poetry", *Lungta* (forthcoming).

Pema Tsering, trans. Riika Virtanen, "The Deceitfully Erected Stone Pillar and the Beginnings of Modern Tibetan Literature", *The Tibet Journal,* Vol.24, No.2, Summer 1999, pp.112-124.

Penick, Douglas J., *The Warrior Song of King Gesar,* Boston: Wisdom Publications, 1996.

Rang grol (Don grub rgyal), trans. Mark Stevenson & Lama Choedak T. Yuthok, "A Threadlike Path", *The Tibet Journal,* Vol.22, No.3, Autumn 1997, pp.61-66.

Roberts, Dexter, "Are You Tibetan or Chinese? Or A Man of the World? Words for Tashi Dawa From a Retired American English Professor" (review of Tashi Dawa's *Soul in Bondage*), *The Tibet Journal* (forthcoming).

Ross, Joanna, *Lhamo: Opera from the Roof of the World,* New Delhi: Paljor Publications, 1995.

Smith, Warren W. Jr., *Tibetan Nation: A History of Tibetan Nationalism and Sino-Tibetan Relations,* Boulder: Westview Press, 1996.

Speyer, J.S., *The Jātakamālā: Garland of Birth-Stories of Āryaśūra,* Delhi: Motilal Banarsidass, 1971 (first Indian edition).

Stevenson, Mark, "Paths and Progress: Some Thoughts on Don grub rgyal's `A Threadlike Path'", *The Tibet Journal,* Vol.22, No.3, Autumn 1997, pp.57-60.

Stoddard, Heather, "Don grub Rgyal (1953-1985): Suicide of a Modern Tibetan Writer and Scholar", in Per Kvaerne (ed.), *Tibetan Studies: Proceedings of the 6th Seminar of the International Association for Tibetan Studies, Fagernes 1992,* Oslo: The Institute for Comparative Research in Human Culture, 1994, pp.825-836.

——, "Tibetan Publications and National Identity," in Robert Barnett and Shirin Akiner, *Resistance and Reform in Tibet,* pp.121-156.

Tashi Dawa, *A Soul in Bondage: Stories from Tibet,* Beijing, Panda Books, 1992.

Yao, Wang, *Tales from Tibetan Opera,* Beijing: New World Press, 1986.

Works in Tibetan Language

Klu 'bum Ye shes rGya mtsho, *Zang zing gi 'jig rten* ("The World of Turmoil"), Kathmandu: Gomang Computer Parkhang, 1996.

Klu smyon Ye shes rGya mtsho, *Sham bha la'i dud sprin* ("The Clouds of Shambhala"), Kathmandu: Gomang Computer Parkhang, 1996.

bKra shis dPal ldan, *"gNyan sgrig"* ("Marriage"), in *Lho kha'i rtsom rig sgyu rtsal,* 1984, No.2, pp.3-18, rTsed thang: Bod ljongs lho kha sa khul rig rtsal lhan tshogs.

——, *"Sems nad"* ("Anxiety"), *sBrang char,* 1986, No.3, pp.12-22.

——, *"Don grub rgyal gyi brtsams 'bras dang des bod rigs kyi rtsom rig gsar par thebs pa'i shugs rkyen skor"* ("On Döndrub Gyel's writings and their influence on the modern Tibetan literature"), *Bod ljongs zhib 'jug,* 1989, No.1, pp.64-85.

——, *Phal pa'i khyim tshang gi skyid sdug,* ("The Joys and Sorrows of an Ordinary Family"), Bod ljongs mi dmangs dpe skrun khang, 1992.

——, *"Yig 'bru gcig kyang med pa'i 'phrin yig cig"* ("A Letter Without a Single Character"), *Bod kyi rtsom rig sgyu rtsal* (*Tibetan Art and Literature*), 1994, No.6, pp.68-73.

——, *"Dri yi bzhon pa"* ("Wind"), *Bod kyi rtsom rig sgyu rtsal* (*Tibetan Art and Literature*), 1996, No.1, pp.42-54.

——, *"dByar kha'i lo ma ser po"* ("The Yellow Leaves of Summer"), *Bod kyi rtsom rig sgyu rtsal* (*Tibetan Art and Literature*), 1996, No.2, pp.28-48.

bKra shis Zla ba, *"Bod ljongs/ rgyun bu'i mdud pa la brgyus pa'i rnam shes"* ("Tibet—A Consciousness Knotted in a Leather Strap"), an unidentified photocopy, with an editorial remark that the story was "selected from *Bod ljongs rtsom rig*", pp.279-323.

——, *"gTsang po'i pha rol na"* ("On the Other Side of the River"), *sBrang char* 1986, No.3, pp.1-12.

sKal bzang Lha mo, *Drang srong bsti gnas kyi rmi lam yun cig,* (*Dreaming at the Sage's Abode: Biographical Sketches of Four Living Tibetan Nuns*), Dharamsala: Amnye Machen Institute, 1999.

mKhas btsun bZang po, *Biographical Dictionary of Tibet and Tibetan Buddhism*, Vol.V, Dharamsala: LTWA, 1973.

Gangs bzhad, *Gangs seng 'tshol du phyin pa* ("In Search of the Snow Lion"), Dharamsala: Tanram Pustak, 1997.

dGe 'dun Chos 'phel, *Ri bo hi ma la'i bstan bcos* ("A Treatise of the Himalaya Mountains") in *dGe 'dun chos 'phel gyi gsung rtsom* ("The Writings of Gedün Chöphel") edited by Chab spel Tshe brtan phun tshogs, Vol.2, Bod ljongs bod yig dpe rnying dpe skrun khang, 1990. Revised edition by T.G. Dhongthog, Bir: Dzongsar Institute, 1991.

'Gyur med (ed.), *Lho yi dri bzhon* ("The South Wind"), (Bod kyi deng rabs rtsom rig dpe tshogs), mTsho sngon mi rigs dpe skrun khang, Zi ling, 1992 (2nd edition, 1994).

sGrol skyid, "*Re ba can gyi mi rigs dang khong tsho'i rkang rjes—<<phyi nyin gyi gnam gshis de ring las legs pa yong nges>> zhes pa'i brtsams sgrung bklags rjes*", ("The People with Hopes and Their Footprints—After reading the story called `Tomorrow the Weather Will Certainly Be Better than Today', *Bod kyi rtsom rig sgyu rtsal,* 1994, No.3, pp.50-54.

rNga ba Tshe rgyam, "*rTsom rig dang 'brel ba'i bod kyi snyan ngag gi skor rob tsam gleng ba*" (A Short Discussion on Tibetan Poetry—A Literary Art"), in *Nor mdzod* ("A Treasury of Jewels"), Sidhpur: the Cultural and Literary Research Centre, Norbulingka Institute, 1997, pp.1-14.

Chab 'gag 'Jam mgon "*sKyo snang gi zlos gar*" ("Melancholic Opera Performance"), *rTsam pa*, 1996, No.1, pp.17-20.

Chos kyi rgyal po nor bu bzang po'i rnam thar phyogs bsgrigs byas pa thos chung yid kyi dga' ston ("The Compiled Life Story of the Religious King Nor bu bZang po—The Celebration for the Minds of the Uneducated"), Dharamsala: Tibetan Cultural Printing Press, 1985 (5th edition).

Chu skyes sGrol ma, *sPrin bral zla ba'i 'dzum rlabs* ("The Smile of a Cloudless Moon"), Dharamsala: Tibetan Cultural Printing Press, 1999.

'Jigs med 'Phel rgyas, "*Nu bo sprul skur ngos bzung rjes*" ("After the Recognition of My Younger Brother as an Incarnated Lama"), *sBrang char,* 1996, No.4, pp.3-49.

lJang bu, "*Sog rus las mched pa'i rnam shes*" ("Consciousness Coming from a Shoulder Bone"), *sBrang char,* 1986, No.2, pp.1-7.

bsTan pa Yar rgyas, "*A ri'i shig*" ("An American Louse"), *Bod kyi rtsom rig sgyu rtsal* (*Tibetan Art and Literature*), 1993, No.6, pp.95-102.

——, *Byang thang gi mdzes ljongs* ("*The Beautiful Region of the Northern Plain*"), Bod kyi deng rabs rtsom pa po'i dpe tshogs (2), Bod ljongs mi dmangs dpe skrun khang, 1995.

——, "*mGo ras kyis btums pa'i bu mo*" ("A Girl With Her Face Concealed by a Scarf"), in bsTan pa Yar rgyas, *Byang thang gi mdzes ljongs,* pp.89-115.

Tshe ring Don grub, "*Ra lo*", *sBrang char,* 1991, No.1, pp.41-58.

——, "*Lam*", ("The Way"), *sBrang char* 1984, No.1, pp.5-11.

——, "*Zla 'od 'og gi zlos gar*" ("A Drama Under the Moon-light"), *sBrang char,* 1986, No.3, pp.27-28, 32.

Don grub rGyal "*Brong stag thang*" ("The Plain of Wild Yak and Tiger"), *sBrang char* 1981, No.1, pp.4-18.

——, "*sPrul sku*" ("Incarnation"), *sBrang char,* 1981, No.3, pp.3-24.

——, "*Sad kyis bcom pa'i me tog*" ("A Blighted Flower"), *sBrang char,* 1982, No.4, pp.6-28 and 1983, No.1, pp.8-29, 47.

Don grub rGyal and Tshe ring Don grub, "*rGyu 'bras med pa'i mna' ma*" ("A Shameless Bride"), *sBrang char,* 1983, No.2, pp.41-55.

Don grub rGyal, "Mi rtag sgyu ma'i rmi lam" ("Impermanent Illusory Dream"), *sBrang char,* 1986, No.1, pp.14-26.

——, *Don grub rgyal gyi lang tsho'i rbab chu dang ljags rtsom bdams sgrig* ("Waterfall of Youth and Selected Writings of Don grub rGyal"), Padma 'Bum (ed.), Dharamsala: Amnye Machen Institute, 1994.

Don grub rGyal, *dPal don grub rgyal gyi gsung 'bum* ("Collected Works of Döndrub Gyel"), edited by Ban kho and bKra rgyal, 6 vols., Beijing: Mi rigs dpe skrun khang, 1997.

Don grub dBang 'bum, "*rTsom rig gi kun ral dus rabs kyi 'phar rtsa*" ("The Garden of Literature—the Pulse of the Century," *sBrang char,* 1991, No.1, pp.1-7.

dMu dge bSam gtan, *Bod du rig gnas dar tshul mdor bsdus bshad pa* ("A Brief Explanation on the Spread of Learning in Tibet"), Si khron: Si khron mi rigs dpe skrun khang, 1982.

Na ga Sangs rgyas bsTan dar, "*rKang lam phra mo la gzhi bcol te gzhung lam chen mor bgrod dgos pa*" ("The Necessity of Proceeding to the Great Avenue Basing Oneself on the Narrow Foot-Path"), *Rang dbang*, p.65.

Padma 'Bum, "*Don grub rgyal gyi mi tshe/ skar mda'—mtshan mo'i nam mkha' 'od kyis gshegs nas yal*" ("The Life of Don grub rGyal: A Shooting Star that Cleaved the Night Sky and Vanished"), in Don grub rgyal, *Don grub rgyal gyi lang tsho'i rbab chu dang ljags rtsom bdams sgrig*.

——, *Mi rabs gsar pa'i snying khams kyi 'phar lding* ("The Heart Beat of the New Generation"), Dharamsala: Amnye Machen Institute, 1999.

dPal ldan rGyal, *mChod* ("Offering"), Dharamsala: Amnye Machen Institute, 1997.

'Phags pa dPa' bo (Āryaśūra), *sKyes pa'i rabs kyi rgyud* (*Jātaka-mālā*), Vol.128, No.5650 in *bsTan 'gyur*, mDo 'grel of *The Tibetan Tripitaka*, ed. Daisetz T. Suzuki, Tokyo-Kyoto: Tibetan Tripitaka Research Institute, 1957.

Bar zhi Phun tshogs dBang rgyal, *gNa' rabs bod kyi chang sa'i lam srol* (*Tibetan Marriage Custom*) Dharamsala: LTWA, 1979.

Be ri 'Jigs med dBang rgyal, *Dus rabs gsar pa'i rtsom rig pa zhig gi snying khams nas 'phos pa'i zungs khrag* ("Blood from the Heart of a Writer of the New Generation"), Mundgod: Drepung Loseling Photo Offset Printers, 1996.

dByangs sgrol, "*Sras mo g.yang skyid sgrol ma*" ("Daughter Yangkyi Dölma"), *sBrang char*, 1996, No.2, pp.1-32.

Rang grol [= Don grub rGyal], "*rTsom rig sgyu rtsal gyi snang brnyan skor cung tsam gleng ba*" ("A Short Discussion on Literary Images"), *sBrang char*, 1982, No.1, pp.48-50.

——, "*Lang tsho'i rbab chu*" ("Waterfall of Youth"), *sBrang char*, 1983, No.2, pp.56-62.

Rang dbang ("Freedom"), Dharamsala: Amnye Machen Institute, 1996.

Rus pa'i rgyan can, *rNal 'byor gyi dbang phyug chen po mi la ras pa'i rnam mgur* ("The Life Story and Songs of the Great Yogi Mi la ras pa"), Dharamsala: Tibetan Cultural Printing Press, 1990.

Sangs dran Bu, "*rGyu 'bras med pa'i mna' ma zhes par dpyad pa mdo tsam brjod pa*" ("A Short Analysis on *The Shameless Bride*," *sBrang char* 1985, No.3, pp.72-79.